Spilled Milk

Spilled Milk

lisha shaffer

To order additional copies of this book, contact:
Xlibris
1-888-795-4274
www.Xlibris.com
Orders@Xlibris.com
788962

Dedicated to my Grannie, Elnora Williams Shaffer

I miss you Grannie Pooh Pooh

INTRODUCTION/ACKNOWLEDGEMENTS

As I sit here at my laptop, trying to think of a conventional way to type this portion of the book, I have to ask myself why. I know and hope that there'll be millions of readers who will pick this book up who doesn't know me on a personal level but getting personal with my readers is the only way that I know how to be. So if I offend anyone who is reading this by not being conventional, I apologize, I think.

I can't begin to express how elated I was when I opened my mail from the Library of Congress (LOC). Not that I needed anyone to verify that my work was an original piece but I now had proof that no one has stolen it along the way and that it is truly an original idea. You know that saying "great minds think alike"? Well, they do; it's just a matter of who's first to express their thoughts to the world that makes a difference.

Opening that letter and seeing my registered work, gave me a sense of accomplishment. Although I registered Spilled Milk with the Writers Guild of America, the LOC just felt much more... thorough.

I am a mother of two beautiful children who are so different from each other but so much like me, in so many ways that it's crazy. We've had our good and bad times just like any other family and I'm sure that I'm not the only mother in the world who has felt like she was the blame for the choices that her children have made but just like other mothers, I had to be confident in the words that God had placed on my tongue for them over the years and digress.

I love my children, Kavonte and Kortnie with all that I am and they have both given me great encouragement during my writing process and not just with this novel but with my poetry, black history programs and with my plays. Kortnie, even though she hasn't read any of my work, is my personal cheerleader with her "Go Mommy you can do it" chants and Kavonte... well; let me put it like this. When you have a teenager (that's when he started reading my stories) ask to read your work, get lost in the story and tell you that "This is really good, I thought this was a real book; where's the rest?" everything in your body that moves will encourage you to keep going. I am truly grateful to God for them.

I've been writing for a long time, even before Ms. Landando's (formerly Mrs. Bates) class, however that Creative Writing class opened up a whole new world of writing for me. Ms. Landando taught me to write short stories from the smell of popcorn, the sound of a cow bell and just from one worded ideas it seemed. I am forever grateful to that woman. She also made us spell her maiden name correctly on a test after her divorce. It's funny now but I learned much later in life, exactly how she felt.

Another woman that I am forever grateful and indebted to is my Mommy, Christina S. Thomas. Just for the record and I must say this, in no way does she comes second to anyone; my thoughts are just pouring out in this order. Those who know me know this for a fact. Smile Mommy.

This woman taught me so many things but most importantly she taught me not to be afraid to tell my stories. It was during a holiday, Thanksgiving I believe, when this Child Development student, my mom, decided to share a story that she did for a class project with "my" friends and I. Just like any teenager, I was too embarrassed to have my parent do anything in front of my friends. I tried to figure out why I was feeling that way but then I thought "my mom is cool, she's never embarrassed me before". So my next thought was that if my friends don't like it, too darn bad.

My mom began to tell her story of the Blue Dog, using cut outs of people and a dog mad of felt paper and placing them on a felt poster board as the story moved along. It was a story of how these children wanted to wash their dog but didn't listen clearly to their parent's instructions. The children washed their dog with blue dye instead of the detergent in a blue bottle, if I'm not mistaken. It was inventive and exciting and no doubt set off sparks in me. Most importantly, at the time, my friends enjoyed it. I was so proud of her; I believe that I am her biggest fan. Thank you, Mommy.

Now for my dad, Al Buford, whose encouragement isn't verbalized as much, can't be slighted. In small ways my dad had and has a huge impact on the progression of my projects and productions. I'm not sure if he knows this and I'm sure he'll say "I knew that" but just by him asking "what's new" when we talked, pushed me to complete a project or a check list at a nice pace.

I'd always make sure that there was something new to tell him by the next time that I spoke to him. Now generally I speak to my Dad once or twice a week, so if I told him that I was working on something, I had to keep it moving. I would work hard to have a different report; a completion of something or even just a positive update. Thank you, Daddy.

Now to my family; many of which has supported me on different levels for different events in my life. My sisters, Toni and Regina, I thank you both for always being there for whatever I need. I promise you, your "I love you sis" text messages always came through at the right time and just knowing that you both are proud of me keeps me moving.

My nieces and nephews; Dionte, Dijon, Dijonnea, Kyndell, Deja, and Monte, you all are just the bomb diggety! Love your energy, your jokes and everything else about you. Thank you for all your support.

Robin and Tyesha, my cousins by birth but my sisters by life, thank you both for your support. Robin, you always make sure that I'm "okay" and that I'm equipped with writing material; like notebooks. Keeping up with multiple pieces of paper can be a bit of a challenge. Tyesha, you've supported me by coming to every event that I've ever had, encouraging me to do whatever would make my heart content. Thank you.

Johnnie and Deborah Shaffer, thank you for your continued support just by showing up. Debra you've given me a notebook or two also but you've trusted me to direct plays for your congregation; that meant more to me than you could imagine. Thank you.

Tyone Maxwell and Rayshawn Sheppard, thank you so much for all the plugs. You may not have been able to make it to a lot of my events but you have been great promoters and that's says a lot. Thanks cousins.

To my Aunts; Linda Sheppard (left me too soon) Queen Ester Shaffer and Janice Benson, I want to thank you all for the support you've given me in one way or another. Rather it was coming to a show, purchasing a ticket or actually working as an usher during an event, all of which is amazing support and love. Thank you.

Thank you Auntie, Carrie Bolden, for always making me feel like a celebrity.

Auntie Barnetta Willard, my amazing and beautiful oldest aunt, thank you so much for all your support. You never tell me that you're going to come to an event or not so when I would see you walk in, it's always a pleasant surprise. Thank you.

Auntie Linda Barrett, thank you for being my "go-to" prayer warrior. I mean my "on the spot" prayer warrior. Before I can finish saying that I need prayer, you're already beginning and it's amazing to feel your words resonating the healing. Thank you.

Marnetta Buford, my youngest aunt, thank you so much for your support. I've only known you for a few years but you stepped into my life as if there had been many.

I can't find the words to express my gratitude to my friends and I don't use that word loosely. I'm sure that I can speak for every artist or anyone that has created a business, by saying our expectations, for those that we know to be supportive, is very high. However, not everyone that we know wants us to succeed.

There are those, and very many, who want to just sit back and see what you can do. The very ones who like to ask "how's it going?" or "when are you going to do something big?" are the ones who never show up. Then you have those who are there in all sorts of ways and are more upset about not "showing up" than you are. There are those who pray for your steps, your health and your mindset and all around wish you the best. There are also those who jump in last minute to fill a character role without much of a complaint. These are the people that I call friends.

So thank you: Armecia Cooper, Raquel Hutchins Curry, Elliott Porter, Kimberly Payne Thomas, Ron Matthews, Anthony Washington, Khary Adams, Bruce Wilson, Barbra Smith, Eric Dixon, Shari Holloway, Darryl

(Jackie) Hammond, Louvenia Clark McMurray, Reggie Haynes, Chante Washington, Basha Evans, Les Wells, Dominique Washington, Deacon Percy and Loretta Hope, Minister Patrick and Deatrice English, Minister Eddie and Letha Gillis, Sister Sneed (6:22 am scriptures) and... I'm sure that I'm forgetting someone. Thank you.

JUST FRIENDS

JUST FRIENDS

The shadows at first were a bit alarming but the bedside tray and curtains became clearer after blinking my eyes a few times. Looking over at Jason, it was hard to tell if he was breathing, but the rise and fall of the bed sheet along the side of the railings answered my question. I've probably checked on him five times last night. And judging by how this blanket is pulled up to my neck, Jason has also checked on me. I've never been able to keep a blanket on me all night; it would either be tangled around my ankles or on the floor. He began to stir in that narrow bed, so I closed my eyes.

"Yeah, like you would sleep past six o'clock". Jason said. I didn't open my eyes but I could hear him fluffing his pillow and adjusting his I.V. cords. "You look crazy over there in that bed" he laughed.

"Not as crazy as you do with that thing up your nose". He laughed softly. We'd been in this hospital for about a month now. I talked the nurses into letting me stay in Jason's room about a week ago; I told them that we had been joined at the hip for twenty years and the separation was killing us. They laughed at me of course, but agreed with one or two conditions; one was that I don't cause them any trouble and two... "Breakfast should be here soon, what did you order?"

"I ordered oatmeal." He paused. "Yes, the way you like it Kori." I smiled under my covers because I knew oatmeal drenched in butter and brown sugar was coming my way. "I had a dream last night" he shouted from the bathroom where I knew he was cleaning his face and brushing his teeth. I was all for cleaning my face before breakfast but toothpaste and oatmeal wasn't a tasty combination.

"About...?" I asked.

"It was about when we first met".

"Was it my version or yours?" I waited for him to spit, rinse and gargle before he answered. He pushed the I.V. pole out of the bathroom and over

1

to me. His color was slowly coming back and he was still a little weak but his smile made him look good.

"There is only one version, the truth." He shook his head at me probably thinking of my version of our first meeting; it involved him being some kind of frog in heat with a bad sense of humor. I laughed at myself.

"Tell it to me again daddy." I snuggled into the not-so-comfortable bed in which I had to make up myself; that was the second condition and waited for Jason to get settled back into bed to tell me a story that I've heard a million times.

"Once upon a time, in a magical kingdom, there lived a beautiful princess with full pouty lips and a big butt." We both laughed at his added detail of the non-truth.

"Come on Jay." I laughed

"Ok. The princess never paid attention to the neighboring prince so one day while she was talking to the King, the Prince sneaked up behind her, placed a magical pouch near her feet and stepped on it. The pouch released sparkling magical powers that made the princess fall in love with him forever."

"Forever"

"And ever" Jason sighed as we both laid there smiling, thinking about what really happened that day. Instead of a magical kingdom, we were in third grade recess, that magical pouch was a package of mustard and the sparkles that splashed all over my powdered blue pants, never washed out. Yes, after chasing him the rest of recess, that moment may have very well started our "forever and ever".

"Good morning, I need to check your vitals Mr. Jason." The heavy set morning nurse rushed in and pulled back the curtains. The pink breast cancer ribbons on her scrubs swayed with every one of her Spanish curves. She turned and looked at me as if trying to remember who I was.

2

"Oh! Good morning, Ms. Kimi." She shook her head at me and smiled. I smiled back, too much in a good mood to correct her on my name.

"Aren't you going to check my vitals as well?"

"I'm sure you're just fine" Nurse Maria continued with Jason.

"I could have a fever or something over here and it'd be your entire fault if something was to happen to me" I whined poking out my lip. Jason gave Nurse Maria the eye then she agreed to take my temperature. I smiled at her then opened wide when she approached my bed.

"No senorita. For an accurate reading, I have to take it from the other end." She stood there smiling with her purple rubber gloves on, squeezing her sausage sized fingers.

"No the heck you're not" I pulled the covers over my head. Nurse Maria and Jason laughed at my expense; Jason over did it a little. His cough, this time, seemed as if it wasn't going to stop. Nurse Maria and I were both at his side waiting, the cough subsided.

"Look at you two. I'm fine and nothing's going to stop me from going home today... well from getting out of here at least." He gave a light laugh.

"Want some water or something?" The nurse asked already pouring water into a foam cup. I didn't move until Jason squeezed my hand letting me know that he was truly ok.

"Ok I'll be back to check on you in about an hour." Nurse Maria yelled over her shoulder as she wiggled out of the room and the breakfast tray rolled in. Jason patted the spot next to him and I took my position. He flicked through the channels before returning to the morning news while I added cream and sugar to my coffee and took the lid off of his orange juice. We ate quietly shaking our heads at the nightly crimes that seems to keep television going.

"I believe reporters only find negative news to purposely make people have a bad day so that they can stir up more trouble. There should be a law against bad news in the morning." I said.

"Sharon will be by here today." Jason said easily as if he was saying the walls in the room were white. I tried to tell myself not to get upset but it wasn't working. Didn't I just say we shouldn't hear bad news in the morning?

"So, what the hell does she want?" Ok that was harsh but I no longer liked the woman and I had no idea why he wanted to see her. "When did you talk to her? Did you call her while I was in the bathroom or something?"

"Are you really going to do this today Kori?" I didn't answer him. I grabbed my robe and walked out. After everything that woman has put him through, he's still giving her the time of day and I'm not going to stick around for it. After I get him some more juice, and a box of Mike & Ike's, his favorite candy, I'm leaving for the day.

THREE MONTHS EARLIER

JASON

"Why you got to eat like that?" Kori was nagging me again. That's like her fifth time tripping on something that I was doing and she wasn't finished. "No wonder you can't keep a woman; you chew like a cow." She frowned at me and then she dug a meatball out of her spaghetti and ate it with her fingers, I shook my head.

"I guess that line of guys forming around the corner is waiting for a chance to dine with 'Lady Koriana'."

"Ha-ha! You are supper funny" she smirked licking her fingers.

"Kori, why you all over me today?"

"Why are you?"

"Why am I what?" She was confusing me.

"That wasn't proper. You said 'why you' instead of why are you..."

"You know what..." I was ready to leave her ass sitting by herself.

"Dude, I'm just joking. Damn. What's wrong with you?" She waited for an answer.

"I'm cool."

"You know we've been married fifty years and you still don't know when I'm joking" Kori smiled innocently.

"We're not married Kori."

"And I'm only thirty. Lighten up brother." She was getting upset. "I'm going to the ladies room so you can take a chill pill, observe the scenery, and have a minute to yourself or whatever." Kori grabbed her purse and left the table. I hate it when she says 'whatever' and she knows this.

She does things that makes you want to shake her and spin her back to normal. Then she can be so sweet you could actually smell the honey. I took a few deep breaths and looked around. It was a nice intimate setting; jazz was playing on the overhead speakers and couples were smiling and laughing, just being real happy with each other.

A nice evening breeze was blowing over and around the buildings from the lake and I was starting to mellow out again. Kori is a little nerve wrecking but she is very caring so I began, again, to appreciate our friendship by the time she arrived back at our table. At that exact moment a very beautiful lady walked up and asked me if she knew me from somewhere. Kori smacked her lips so loud that the lady looked at her. To her surprise, the lady asked Kori the same question and I immediately recognized her from high school. Kori puts on her fake bourgeois attitude and asked without even looking at the woman, "Where would we know you from."

"She went to school with us; they used to call you 'Pinky' right?" I stood up and gave her a hug. Kori looks up at us with a phony smile planted on her face.

"Oh I remember you. You used to date Kelvin, no Derrick or was it Samson? I can't remember which. Or did you date all of them?" Kori was really being rude.

"Your name is James right?" Pinky asked me, unsure of my name, but totally ignoring Kori.

"His name is Jason sweetie."

"Oh yeah" Pinky shifts awkwardly from her left foot then to the right. Kori was staring at her intensely.

"I heard that the two of you were still the best of friends but I had no idea that you were..."

"Yes, we are" Kori interrupted.

"Have you all been together since high school or is this..."

"Yes."

"Do you all have any children?"

"No."

"Want any?"

"Yes."

"No" I finally found my way back into the conversation. They were going back a forward like a game show or something. I didn't understand Kori's reason but I couldn't call her a liar in front of a practical stranger either. Pinky said her good-byes and we were alone again. "Why did you do that?" I stared at Kori eating apple pie and ice cream as if nothing happened.

"Didn't you tell me that you were serious about Sharon?" She asked. Yes is my reply but I also told her "that's my business though". She swallowed some milk and say...

"Okay fine. I won't hang out with her anymore and tell her not to call me either." She waits for my reply.

"Now why you have to act like that?" Kori slowly put down her fork and looked me square in the eyes. She explained, in her motherly tone, how women talk about men, comparing notes and how she couldn't possibly continue to honestly tell Sharon that I'm a good man if I'm out here flirting with every skirt with legs that smiled at me.

"It would be different if I didn't like Sharon." Kori ended laying her fork on the table and crossed her arms. At this point, I was starting to smell the honey riding in the wind. Although I wasn't flirting, not yet anyway, I was embarrassed. So I did what men do best at moments like these, I changed the subject. "She didn't even remember my name" I laughed.

"Didn't you do her under the bleachers? Yes you did" She tells my shaking head as I laughed, remembering that game against King. We all won that day. "Why did the boys call her pinky?"

"I don't know" I lied. Inside jokes for men are meant to stay inside jokes for men.

"Well, as black and ashy as she was, you all should have called her 'dusty'. We both fell out laughing. After Kori paid the check we took a cruise down Lake Shore Drive, bumping some Jazz as we headed south, Kori insisted on driving so she could have control of the radio. I glanced over at her and she had this pleasant look on her face, something I've never seen on the faces of the women I dated. I wondered if she was seeing someone new, so I asked.

"What's with the look?"

"I'm just thinking" she said as her smile brightened.

"It must be good" I said. She said nothing. "What-are-you-thinking" I said slowly with some fake sign language to get a laugh out of her. It works.

"I'm thinking about how it would feel to know you forever." Kori smiled at me and I felt a strange rush of heat flood my soul. So I turn from her and for the very first time in our lives, I didn't know what to say to my best friend.

KORI

Why is it that my best dates are with Jason? I didn't get in until two this morning. We drove from downtown, South on Lake Shore Drive and then back North again. Jay was sitting kind of quiet so I popped in a mix CD and fast forwarded it to Ray Foxx, the "Trumpeter". I pulled over to the shoulder, turned Jason's Bose speakers up to the max, walked to the passenger side, opened the door and asked "may I have this dance?" He first expressed how crazy I was before getting out of the car to dance with me. We danced that whole song and then the next two. The last dance was slow. Dancing with Jason was comfortable and safe, with no worries of someone grabbing my ass, or trying to take me home for the night.

We even had cars blowing their horns at us as they passed by. It was a great evening and that's why I'm late for church. Well that and pushing the snooze button for two hours and listening to twelve voice messages; one of which was a message from Sharon, Jason's girlfriend. I truly believe that woman calls me more than Jason does, probably living by that rule "keep your friends close, and your enemies closer". She's pretty cool, I guess, no kids, good job; most of what Jason is looking for in a woman. The phone ranged and I knew it was her.

"Hello." I tried to sound busy.

"Hey girl, this is Sharon. Did you get my message about the Black Women's Expo?"

"Hey Sharon, I did get your message but I was just heading out the door. Can you call me on my cell phone?"

"I just want to confirm really quickly that you're going." She didn't give me much of a chance to think about it. Hanging with her was no problem because I'd learned to block out her sneer remarks about people, but to be surrounded by her and her friends was going to be a challenge. I told her that I'd go and that she could pick me up at one O' clock, looked in the mirror and decided to change clothes, there was no way that I was wearing a flower print dress to the expo. I braced myself for my mother's disapproving looks of the dress I changed into.

Sharon and I road practically in silence; outside of Jason, we didn't have much in common. Sharon being a mere three years older, we barely had music in common. After discussing who was using who in the celebrity world and an informal update on Jason, the radio kept us company all the way to the McCormick Place.

Sharon's friends were at the front entrance waiting when we arrived. The three of them were decked out in various colored skirt suits, they were too 'business' like for my taste. This made me so glad to have worn my blue knit dress showing much cleavage and my cropped leather jacket, I love to be different. And by the expression on the taller friend's face, she didn't appreciate me being different.

"I thought Sharon said you were coming from church?" The tall one said looking me up and down over the rim of her glasses.

"I did." I told her while adjusting the gold infinity scarf around my neck.

"You're looking kind of sexy for church?"

"Oh is that why all the single guys were looking at me." I said to the tall one, in which I later learned was named Myra.

"Girl, at my church 'they'd' look at you so hard, you'd want to go home and change." Myra said trying to make her statement sound like a joke.

"Well" I said as I removed my gold leather gloves, "'they' usually mean 'females' and I'm the last person in Chicago who would care what a female thought of what I'm wearing." Except for my mother in which I received an ear full. I smiled at Myra as if to say 'even you', Myra said nothing.

I guess Sharon felt the heat because she began to introduce everybody, hellos went out respectively and we began our journey. Most of them went to school with her but I remember her mentioning that Myra worked with her and after a half hour of listening to gossip I was grateful to see an ex-boyfriend of mine who wanted the 411 on my last two years, I didn't hesitate to tell 'the girls' that I'd catch up in a few moments.

"I see you have a new set of friends, not your type though." Kevin was still gorgeous, but I wouldn't dare tell him that.

"I know and no they're not my friends. One is Jason's girlfriend and the others are her friends." I said glancing over my shoulder at 'the girls'. Kevin faked a look of astonishment.

"You're rolling with one of Jay's women. Que lest ce monde 'a venir. What is the world coming to?" He slapped a hand to his forehead and I laughed, I was amazed myself.

"This one's a lot better than the last ten, she can actually read." We laughed as we glanced over some pamphlets from an A.M. radio station.

"You really don't give them a chance Kori; as soon as you meet them you judge them." Kevin placed an arm around my shoulder as if to soften what he'd just told me.

"Do I?" He nodded yes. "I don't think so; see the difference between men and women is that we can see the defects in people or in men right away. Some women chose to ignore them but we see them. Men, you all don't see the defects until you sleep with a woman or loan a guy some money. Some of you are so blind you can't see anything wrong until after the wedding."

"You know you're still crazy." He joked, I smiled. "So what was my defect?" Kevin asked stopping to face me. I thought for a moment, I really didn't want to spoil the moment by telling the truth so I said 'bad timing' on his part. He was sexy, a great kisser, great in bed and he could cook. I wanted to tell him so but I felt that standing in the middle of the Black Women's Expo wasn't a proper place to discuss something so personal.

"Are you here alone?" I asked as I looked around to see if some woman was off to the side 'mean mugging' me.

"No not really, Mike and Tim are here female hunting."

"And you're not?" I raised my eyebrows.

"I guess you could say that I'm doing a little window shopping also." He gave me the sexiest 'I like what I see' kind of look. It worked, I couldn't stop smiling.

"Well, I'll tell you this; if you could get me away from the 'want to be house wives of Chicago' I'll give you an answer to your question." I challenged.

"Easy!" Kevin needed no further persuading. He walked me over to Sharon and her friends, told them that I was leaving with him and led me towards the exit. I gladly waved at the four surprised faces I was leaving behind.

Kevin gleefully called his boys on his cell phone, as we walked to his five year old black Lexus; he believed in preserving the good things. "I take care of her she takes care of me" Kevin announced as he held the door for me. I watched his long body move around to the drivers' side, long graceful strides. Then he smiled my way exposing a very deep dimple-that dimple was the very reason I talked to him in the first place. That dimple and those juicy lips made me want all of him two years ago. Kevin skin was perfect; there were no blemishes or hair bumps and he was never ashy looking. Just makes a woman want to touch him all day long.

I wish that I was more stable when we were dating. I had bills up the 'wha-zoo', school and work to juggle and a man fine as Kevin needed my full attention and a little more. I didn't have time to be 'somebody's woman'. He was striving to be a celebrity sports agent and his needs off the road were a bit much for me.

Now my credit is in the seven hundreds (middle score at that), I have my Master's from Columbia and I'm head of my own advertising team for the second largest advertising agency in Chicago. I am also bored and my social life has taken a downward slide to a land of inactivity. And like my Assistant Minister says "inactive means dead."

My outings with Jason, once a month, just aren't enough. I thought about taking on some duties at the church but every time I'm prepared, mentally, the company calls demanding immediate attention from my team. I guess that could be considered a blessing, but fitting in the Lord's work has become a very hard task. I really need to flip the script.

"You're taking me home?" I asked Kevin as the sight of my apartment building drew me out of my private thoughts.

"Well, I thought we would go to your place, talk a few minutes and then I'd be out. That way you'd already be home." He had the nerve to smile, as if that was a good idea.

"I could have taken a cab home if I wanted to go home."

"My fault" he threw his hands up in submission. "You didn't say where you wanted to go you just said to get you out of there." Kevin was right; I hadn't given him any directions and that was another reason I didn't have time for him. I had to do all the thinking and the planning when it came to us. He could plan small trips for potential ball players in a heartbeat but when it came to "Kori" it was always up to me. Fine! I'll let him in this time but if he invite himself over again then he's in for a big surprise.

Once inside the apartment, Kevin took his shoes off at the door. Although my carpet is a light gray, he knew that I didn't like dirt tracked inside. I took our coats and hung them in the closet then proceeded to take off my boots. Before I could unzip the first boot Kevin had stooped down to help me. Watching him pull off my boots made me remember how attentive he was. He took my hand and led me to my charcoal gray leather sofa as if I was a guest in his house. Kevin looked out at Lake Michigan for a moment then turned to face me. I took my cue and told him my side of the story. You know, about my bills and stuff and when I was done he seemed pleased that it wasn't totally his fault.

"So! What now?" Kevin asked.

"What? You mean now that I'm straight?" I was unsure of his question so I waited for an explanation.

"I mean, you're done with school and your finances are more than straight" he took my hand in his. "Can we pick this back up?" I didn't expect him to be so eager to jump back into my life. Although I wouldn't mind seeing him again, I was always taught that something easily gained was not worth having.

"We could date." I said rising to walk into the kitchen for a drink of water. "Want some juice or something?" Kevin was now standing behind me.

"Does dating mean we could do this" Kevin placed his arms around my waist. I nodded yes. "What about this" he put his full lips on the back of my neck. I nodded yes. I knew then that I should stop him but I didn't. He turned me around and gave me the deepest, warmest and most sensual kiss ever. I began to feel tingles between my toes and other places that had an in between as Kevin pressed against my body. His hands felt like a heat lamp as he rubbed my back and my hips.

How long has it been since my body had been touched so passionately? I have no idea but this was getting out of hand. Kevin hands were busy trying to undo my dress while his lips were undoing my cool. Stop. Stop. I tried to say out loud but a lump of desire was stuck in my throat. Kevin had succeeded in removing my dress and was in the process of lifting my shaking body to the kitchen counter before I could even exhale. He began to speak French; naming my body parts as he kissed them. He kissed my forehead "front", my nose "Nez", my chin "menton" and then he kissed my neck saying "cou". I was still keeping it together until he got to my mouth saying "bouche" and then the middle of my chest "poitrine" but when he got to my thighs and said "cuisse" which would always sound like "kiss" to me and then I could never help but to repeat after him, making him kiss it again; that's when I almost lost it.

"Let me think" I thought. I wanted to stop him just on principle but I needed him to keep going because… well, I needed him to keep going. But how would I look in the long run? What if he just wanted to get some for old time sake? I really needed to get a grip. "Kevin?" I called his attention from the crest of my navel.

14

"Yeah baby" he stood up, kissed me and then he let me breathe again.

"You're going beyond dating." There, I said it. I may have been a little horny but I had to be smart too. I had to see where he was at with all this 'let's start over' stuff.

"I just wanted you to know how much I missed you" he kissed my forehead and helped me down from the counter. "I hope you're up for a game of 'gin rummy' cause I miss doing that with you as well." Just like that, Kevin had regained his composer while I needed a cold shower and a horror flick to make me forget what just happened. But I was glad that I didn't have to fight him off; that would have ended the 'us thing' right then and there.

JASON

"Jay you should have seen her" Sharon was happily explaining to me how Kori was swept off her feet by some guy at the expo.

"Who was he?" I asked suddenly feeling a sickness in the pit of my stomach.

"I don't know boo. But brother man was super fine." I threw Sharon a look as to say 'have you forgotten who you're talking to'. I guess she figured it was ok since she was referring to someone who wasn't putting interest in her.

"He didn't look better than you sweetie." Sharon tried to cover up her statement by kissing me on the back of my shoulder. I was standing in my closet picking out some clothes to wear to an art show the next day. I'd chosen a navy suit, a royal blue shirt and a beige and blue print tie Kori bought for me last week. It was one of her 'just because' presents, as if she needed a reason to shop. It seemed as if all my ties were from Kori; the red one with the royal blue dots, the green one, the black with gray stripes, in fact, from what I could see at least ten of them were from her.

Sharon was still going on and on about dude. How tall he was, how smooth he was dressed and how happy, again, Kori was to be leaving with him. She was beginning to piss me off for some reason.

"Why are you so happy about it?" I kind of yelled but I didn't mean for it to come out like that, but it did.

"No reason." Sharon sat up from lying across my bed. "Why are you so angry about it" she snapped. I wasn't expecting that.

"I'm not angry but you act like Kori never had a man before." I tried to sound defensive for Kori's sake instead of showing what I was really feeling, in which I wasn't certain.

"Well she hasn't had one since I've known her." Sharon said pulling off her shoes.

"Well some women don't need to have back to back men to make them feel complete." Damn! That slipped and Sharon froze. Kori told me never to use a woman's past relationship as a weapon. That is if I wanted to keep her and as far as I knew, I wanted to keep Sharon. When Sharon and I started dating she confided that she has never been without a man, her longest grace period being a week long. Strange as it may seem, I took that as a challenge instead of a red flag.

Sharon didn't say a word; her jaw set tight, shoulders stiffened, and with quick harsh shoves her shoes were back on her feet and the spot where she was laying was now empty. I asked her where she was going but she didn't respond. I knew she was hurt but I couldn't take it back.

"Sharon!" She didn't answer again. So I followed her into the living room where I found her putting on her coat. "Why are you leaving Sharon?"

"You know why." Here we go with the games. Why do women like to torture the brothers? "Just answer the question." I stood by the door so she couldn't get out.

"Could you move Jason?" Sharon looked at me with a look of hatred. Instantly I'd become every ex-boyfriend she's ever had. I was Tommy the cheater, Greg the manipulator and Steve who actually never did anything wrong but had absolutely no interest in anything that she wanted to do. Yeah, I agree, women shouldn't tell us about their past relationships.

"Answer the question."

"Move!"

"So you think standing there with rocks in your jaws is supposed to scare me?" I smiled trying to ease the tension in the air. Her lip quivered from what I thought was going to be a laugh but she began to cry. It wasn't a break down kind of cry but an 'I'm fed up' kind of cry. So I did the manly thing and held her. Besides, I hate to see a woman cry so holding her, shielded her face from mine. After she was done she pulled away from my embrace.

"Jason could you move? Please." She didn't look at me this time so I moved to the side and opened the door. I watched her get in her car and take off. Not a glare, a wave of the hand or even the flip of a bird came from her direction. Before I knew it I was on the phone with Kori trying to gain some understanding.

"I would tell you 'I told you so' but I'm not."

"Then what was that Kori?" I knew I shouldn't have called her.

"That wasn't an 'I told you so', I told you so. I said that I wasn't going to say that. But I will say that just because Sharon left doesn't mean it's over. Most women put it in writing or a definite verbal and Sharon would have definitely verbalized it" Kori laughed.

"Why are you laughing?" This was not a funny moment.

"I was just thinking of a definite verbal I gave this one guy a few months ago." she laughed again.

"Hey, who was the dude you met today? The tension that was beginning to fade was put on pause.

"You mean who did I see today? I saw Kevin." She sung his name out to me.

"Sports agent Kevin?" My tension was beginning to return, not because of Kevin; who always gave me tickets to any game happening in the city, but for some other reason that I just couldn't put my finger on.

"So that's why you're so giddy."

"I ain't giddy!" she giggled.

"Yeah, whatever."

"Whatever? Jason's using a word he hates." I can feel her smile getting brighter through the phone, her dimple seeping even deeper. She wasn't even here but I had a clear vision of her in front of me.

"Look man; call Sharon just to see if she made it in safe. Don't try to talk about what happened unless she starts up the conversation. Let her soak a minute and call her before you go to bed tomorrow." Kori's parental voice was on again.

"Yes ma'am." I teased her.

"I'm for real Jay, listen to me for once. Oh and wear the dark blue suit with the gray, blue and black tie and your gray shirt tomorrow, now get some rest chump." She blew me a kiss and hung up. I cleared my line and dialed Sharon's number. The phone rang six times but there was no answer. I looked at my clock and noticed that it had only been twenty minutes since she'd left so she was probably still upset. Now if I was sending a text, she'd be responding with six damn pages of nagging.

I finished preparing my clothes for a long day at the Art Institute's Design department. I've been there for about seven years and it has been very profitable. It seems like just yesterday I was standing in front of DeVry College having my last look as a student. I've gone back a couple of times to give speeches to freshman classes but that's about it.

After I showered, brushed my teeth and oiled myself down, I trimmed my beard and sideburns. Kori says I look older with a beard but I say that I look good. I picked up the phone and dialed Sharon again; she still didn't answer so she was probably screening her calls and didn't want to talk to me. Well, she didn't have to screen them any longer; I wasn't calling her back. She was just going to have to call *me* when she was ready. I turned the television on to watch the game.

KORI

A week had gone by since I'd seen or heard from Kevin. Remember him? You know the one who asked me if we could begin again. Yes, that one. Anyway, that next evening, which was Monday, I called him, in spite of the fact that I only had a cell phone number I called anyway. I hate calling cell phones. I got the voicemail but I didn't leave a message.

Tuesday I called and didn't leave a message. I called Wednesday morning and left a message. Thursday, Friday and Saturday I was too busy gluing Sharon and Jason back together that I'd forgotten all about Kevin and his neglect. That was until I'd taken a soothing vanilla almond bubble bath while I listened to the Isley Brothers and finished off a very large glass of red wine. I had started to feel... well you know where I'm going with this. I had just climbed into bed to watch a comedy to combat my twitching when my doorbell chimed. Guess who? Yes it was Mr. Neglect. So I buzzed him in and grabbed my robe. Not my terry cloth robe but my short, never stay closed, don't you wish you could have some, silk robe. A robe used strictly for torture of course. When I opened the door he grabbed me like I was a long lost friend or something.

"Girl you don't know how much I've missed you." he moaned in my ear. I pushed him to the side and closed the door before we'd started giving my neighbors a show.

"Really? I couldn't tell." I said as I walked over to the window. He didn't seem to catch my attitude which was a good thing. That meant that he wasn't expecting negativity. Which could have also meant that he hadn't done anything negative enough to expect an attitude from me?

"I did. I've been so busy recruiting this week it's crazy. We have commercials and promotions going on left and right." I saw him removing his shoes and his coat through the reflection in the window.

"I've been moving this week too and I lost my cell phone somewhere. I couldn't call you because you didn't give me your number before I left last week." Oops! That was true. I never gave him my number. He could have lost his cell phone but I haven't changed my work location. He could have called me at work. "I was hoping you'd call me at my office or something. You don't believe that I'm for real do you? I guess I could have called you at work but I had so much on my mind and so many things to sort out; this week has been too crazy." he shook his head as he rubbed my feet. At this point, I was sitting on my chaise with my legs crossed at the ankles; beginning to feel punished.

"Care to talk about it." I asked trying to get the sensation that was creeping up my legs off my mind. I also wanted to know how honest he could be.

"I do but not right now. I promise that I'll tell you everything as soon as I have everything under control."

"Why do men feel that they're the ones controlling things down here?"

"We know we don't control anything, we just do our best to keep on top of things instead of under them. You know, so whatever comes up we can be on it." He paused. "Now" he said as he grinned down at me. "I got a surprise for you." He pulled me up from the chaise and into his chest. My breast was against his very hard chiseled chest, and my senses were inhaling his natural aromas straight into my wanting areas. He looked so damn sexy I hoped the surprise was him, but I was wrong.

"Put on some clothes" he said as he pushed me towards my bedroom.

"Why?"

"We have to go outside for it." I looked at the clock, it was almost eleven. Damn! No sex and I'm missing my movie, this had better be good I thought. I threw on a pair of jogging pants and a sweat shirt as ordered. I put on my jacket and gym shoes as we took the elevator down to the lobby. Kevin grinned all the way to the car.

"This must be a really good surprise" I said.

"I'll put it to you this way; it's something I always wanted to give you." He unlocked the car door but he didn't open it. "Close your eyes." I did. He opened the door and guided me into the front seat. Then I heard bells and something crawled from the back of the car, onto my lap and started licking my hands. I jumped of course but when I opened my eyes I found a beautiful black and brown German Shepherd happy to see me.

"Oh Kevin she's gorgeous." I picked the puppy up to let her lick my face.

"Look again beautiful, she's a "he". I can't deal with two females going through "PMS' he laughed.

"Kevin, you know I can't have a dog in this building."

"I know, but I can have whatever I want in my house."

"I don't understand." I got out of the car with my puppy.

"Look!" he pointed to the dog's collar. It had three gold keys hanging from a gold plated key ring that read "Trust". "You can come see him anytime you like."

"You're giving me keys to your new house?" Ok, this was not what I expected. I wondered what all this meant. Were we sharing a house or just sharing a dog? Pets were like children, was he asking me to share a child with him?

"Yeah, is something wrong with that? You're the only woman I've ever wanted to spend my life with." Kevin pulled me into a hug with the puppy between us. "I would be lying if I said that there had been no other women over the past couple of years but they meant nothing." I looked at the key chain and read the address engraved in it and decided to ride the trust wave out. "Do you think that you can handle me now?"

"I guess I'll find out sooner or later."

"I won't disappoint you" he said with a serious face then he gave me one of those long juicy kisses of his. We kissed so long I'd forgotten about the puppy until he started yelping at us. On that note we parted. I headed to my apartment with my new keys in hand, Kevin and 'my' puppy headed home. Why do men always give you gifts that they can play with too?

JASON

"Baby, are you listening to anything that I'm saying?" Sharon was asking me, again, if I was listening. Not hearing her but "listening". I just looked up at her. First of all, I was working on a very difficult part of a painting and her very presence was disturbing me. Second, I hadn't talked to her in almost two weeks since she left my apartment, yet again after a simple misunderstanding, a habit she seem to not want to get rid of. She never wants to talk anything out as if our problems were going to be solved through silence and distance.

She came over teary eyed and pouty, after Kori already told me that she had to convince her to talk to me, dramatically professing her love and how much she's missed me. Sharon took the paint brush out of my hand and started kissing and feeling every part of me, softening my emotional places and hardening others. I was just about to take her into the bedroom when Kori's voice popped into my head. "If you break up or separate from a woman for more than two weeks, and she come back all horny and bothered, do your damnedest... if that's a word, not to sleep with her. It could be a set up. And if you do, which you probably will, do not and I repeat, do not let her supply the condoms. You do use condoms right?"

"What are you laughing at?" Sharon looked up from kissing me in between my thigh and and my groin. Although she tried to hide it, Sharon was disgusted with my interruption. She tried to continue.

"Let's go for a walk."

"A walk" Sharon jumped up and started to re-dress.

"What are you mad at now?"

"Well Jason, only that I'm coming on to you, practically putting your... your... you know what in my mouth and you know I don't like doing that and all you can say is "let's take a walk". She was heading towards the door and I was about to let her turn the knob and get the hell out when I heard myself say "If you leave don't bother to come back." I know it was kind of dramatic right. Actually, that was female-ish. Anyway, what's out is out.

Sharon froze and without turning around she asked me to repeat myself. I know it was a challenge to either bring out the punk in me or the man in me. I thought about the weeks that she'd put between us; the many nights I've endured without you know what, and decided that, "yes I meant it damn it". She turned slowly, walked towards me and sat at the end of the bed. "Ok Jason" she simply said. I looked at her for a long time and wondered if I had made a mistake. I should have let her ass leave.

"Do you have to clank your fork to your plate every time that you put it down?" That was her first time saying something to me since we'd left the apartment. She'd been talking at me and around me but not directly to me. We walked from my apartment to the Lake and back to a coffee shop on fifty-first and Harper and decided to get a bite to eat. I tried to start conversations only to be shot down by her 'really' and dramatic 'wow's and 'oh joy's', so I stopped and let her have her silence. She was so beautiful, much too pretty to have an attitude like this. She wore a weave but she had really nice hair underneath and her skin and nails were perfect. And her body, oh my god, how can I put it. I'll just say she takes very good care of her body.

"You know I've been watching that couple over there." She paused to make sure that I was listening. I was. "I'm sure those aren't her kids." I asked "how do you know". "I know because, the father and the kids are doing most of the talking like they're filling her in on something; filling her in on them. And look at the way they are dressed." I did. "They are clearly Muslim right." I looked them over and thought that she could be right. The children had dreads that needed attention, all three of them were; in jeans, faded t-shirts with some kind of catch phrase wording or Bob Marley, afro centric bracelets and gym shoes that needed soap. Not so much conforming to the celebrity world. Their spirits were very lively and they smelled of incense. They may not have been Muslims, Jamaican maybe but they were definitely clinging tight to their roots. "And look at her; perm, wedge heels, fake nails and leggings. I'm assuming they just started dating and she's underestimated his life style or she wouldn't have worn that I'm sure."

It's amazing how she can come up with such things. She can analyze all of that but can't discuss with me simple misunderstandings; an unanswered text message, slightly late for a dinner date or bringing her coffee instead of a latte. "It's sad though." Ok I wasn't listening that time, what was she talking about now. She continued, "They're going to date for a while, she'll slowly come out of the up-due she's in; heels will reduce to flats, the gel will come off the nails, it will take a good minute for her to come out of that weave though. She'll go natural in a couple of years, but by that time he'll be tired of asking her to come to the temple for worship and sister Betty Shabazz or somebody will have his attention. Then that's when she'll ask herself "who am I?""

"Your Sharon Sinclair, everyone knows that." Kori was standing there smiling so sweetly behind Sharon and Kevin was closely behind. She hadn't even told me that she was seeing him again but here they were grinning like new pennies. "Hey Jay" she came around to my side of the table and kissed me lightly on the lips. I inhaled her breath and I could almost taste her sweetness. She grinned at me as Kevin pulled out the chair next to me, for her.

"What's up Jay? Long time, no see man." Kevin shook my hand.

"Everything is good. I... um, see you hanging with this bean head so you must be bored." I joked feeling nervous. Or was I feeling jealous? I was a little confused. Why would I feel jealousy?

"Awe, Kori is a lot of fun." He winked at Kori as he pulled up a chair from the next table blocking the isle. His hand was caressing her thigh as if it belonged to him. I wondered if it was soft in that area. I mentally shook my head. Snap back Jason, I told myself.

"Is she really? Hi I'm Sharon." Sharon leaned unnecessarily into him to shake his hand. Kori gave me a side glance and I nodded my head to let her know that "yes I saw that". "I'm Jason's girlfriend, and you are? I didn't get a chance to meet you at the Expo so..."

"Kevin Spade and I am Kori's boy toy." They laughed as if Kevin Hart was telling the joke. I didn't get it. I couldn't imagine someone else kissing

Kori's forehead besides me. Or rubbing her feet, watching movies with her or any of the things that we do... I'm losing it. Kori's had a man before now. What is wrong with me?

"Did you hear me Jason?" Sharon was looking at me blankly.

"No, what did you say?"

"She said 'what's wrong with you'?" Kori was smirking. I knew exactly what she was thinking, Sharon was bossy.

"I said are you ready to order?" Sharon pointed towards the menu. No I wasn't ready to do anything but leave. I was starting to feel sick; I wanted to go home alone, because there, I wouldn't be sitting across from a woman whose importance I was beginning to question or next to one whom I was crazy about. Ok, there, I said it. The truth was out.

KORI

I don't know what Jason was thinking about today, but something was clearly bothering him. Every time Kevin paid me a complement, he would grunt. And when Sharon was speaking he ignored her, when normally he's all ears. I know this to be true because that was the first thing that bothered me about her, the attention he gave her in my presence; he knows that I'm spoiled. Anyway, Kevin and I didn't eat with them because Jason was doing way too much spacing out and Sharon was flirting too obviously, trying to make Jason jealous. I understood her game however she needed to find another victim before she became one. So I helped them out by excusing Kevin and I from their table.

Sharon; extended her two karat diamond ring, gold bangle right hand to Kevin while her left hand played with a strand of "mother of pearl" pearls around her neck and she dramatically crossed her legs, flashing her tan Ralph Lauren Jephina calfskin sandal, all while expressing how "awful it is for you to be leaving so soon, Kevin". Jason almost broke his glass throwing his spoon down at that point. I've never been the jealous type so I wasn't sure how Kevin was receiving Sharon's flirting, but I can tell that he was tickled pink about it. And I'm sure that if Jason had any idea how expensive Sharon's accessories were, he'd run to the hills before wedding bells started ringing in the sweetheart's ears.

Enough about them, let's get back to Kevin and I. We were originally on our way to buy some furniture for "our home", as he like to say, before we saw those two love birds. I like shopping with Kevin because he values and trust my taste in decorating and mainly because he hand over his wallet. That's the best part, not that I would go crazy with the spending but the part about him trusting me with it at all. We entered the store, the salesman stepped to us and the fun began.

"Would you like a round or a square table?" he said.

"Round"

"Would you prefer leather or vinyl seats?"

"I want leather, of course."

"Bar table or..."

"Standard" I cut him off. My legs were too short to sit comfortably on a bar stool for the length of a dinner. "Oh, wait a minute." I noticed a square set of leather bar stools. They were beautiful with cherry wood legs to match the table and the leather cushions were a deep olive green. They would go perfect with his floor tile. "I changed my mind. You have to get this set here."

"You see why I need you?" Kevin was smiling as if he'd just met me. I guess some things are better the second time around. Now Kevin has more time for me, includes me in on his business adventures and he even asks my opinion on some of the players when we're watching a game. The sex is even better. Somewhere along the line of our two year separation, he's learned that he's not the only one who enjoys a good rump around. I'm not even wondering who taught it to him either because I'm the benefactor at the moment.

"Honey can you handle the paper work from here, I need to return a call?" I said sure and Kevin stepped to the side with his cell phone in hand. I don't know who he was calling but I'm sure it was a female because he was smiling too much. I guess we all do that, smile when talking to the opposite sex. Kevin talked during the whole sales transaction. He was quietly pacing when I was filling out the delivery form and he was boastfully laughing when I was checking his schedule, sent via his travel agent to my email on a weekly basis, to choose a delivery date. He was still on that same call when he came over to authorize his credit card and the only part of the conversation I could pick up on at that point was that sometime this week he was "going to be there". I didn't notice anything social on his schedule.

When I finished up I glided over to the bedroom section. Kevin's bed was brand new but mine at my apartment needed an upgrade. After sleeping on Kevin's sleep number mattress, nothing else was good enough. Kevin sneaked up behind me and wrapped his arms around my waist, brushing my left nipple with his thumb. I looked around to see if anyone was watching before I started to enjoy it. No one was even in the area.

"You know what that does to me" I moaned.

"Yes."

"And you're going to do me like this in the middle of this store." My eyes were closed and nothing else mattered but the sway of his thumb and the softness of his lips on the back of my neck. I think if I gave Kevin the opportunity, he would gladly get my off in public.

"There's a bed right here in front of us." See, I told you. I was just about to call his bluff when an elderly sells woman walked up. Now I'm embarrassed. Why couldn't she have been a young horny college kid asking us if we wanted the key to the employees restroom or something. Instead we got someone's grandmother looking at us as if we needed a sex education class.

"I'm sure this mattress would be very comfortable for you two." She touched the mattress as if it were a hot potato. "We get a lot of nice couples in here who can't help but to try out our products." She smirked and began to walk away. She was a jazzy looking grandma switching away in her brown orthopedic loafers.

"What did she call me?" I joked with Kevin when she was out of ear shot.

"She called you a horny toad young lady. She probably got a radar signal from your nipples and ran over here thinking you were in distress." He laughed; I nudged him with my elbow.

"She's probably thinking that for real. What's next on the list?" I wanted to change the subject because there was some truth to grannies thoughts.

"Let me see..." Kevin started circling me while rubbing his chin. "I guess you could go to dinner in that." Ok he was talking about dinner at twelve noon. "Let's fly to Charleston and have dinner." Kevin was excitedly pulling me towards the front entrance of the store.

"South Carolina? Kevin it's too hot for these pants in Charleston." I was referring to the nylon type business slacks that I was wearing. Why was I wearing them anyway on a Saturday?

"I know babe, but they're perfect for a first class flight. We can buy the rest when we land." I was supper excited, finally living out one of my dreams; where a handsome guy spontaneously offer to fly me somewhere for dinner, buying whatever I needed along the way. I hoped he wasn't talking about airport shopping either.

And he wasn't, for as soon as we landed, the limo he ordered before we boarded, was out front waiting for our arrival. The driver holding up a huge sign reading "Mr. Spade" in bold black letters over his head, quickly took us to Towne Centre Mall in Mount Pleasant. Although I love shopping, it is always better when someone else was spending. I've always wanted to come here, but the first chance I got to have a nice vacation, I went to Jamaica instead. The homes along the coast were awesome with their tiered porches and the church steeples standing tall like personal decorations for the city. The town looked ancient and new at the same time.

We passed a water fountain that looked like a giant pineapple had exploded and the bridge over Silicon Harbor looked like spider webs were holding it up. And the lagoons or designer swamps is what I called them, looked like a scene from the Little Mermaid. I felt like a child with my faced pressed against the limo window. We began to drive to a house that looked like a mansion you'd find on the finest soil in Mexico. The drive up entrance was huge and before the car came to a stop, a very plump woman and an elderly man, who appeared to be a butler, was at our door ready to greet us.

"Welcome, Ms. Kori. Welcome to our..."

"What's with the formalities here?" Kevin interrupted the round woman.

"This is absolutely beautiful." I said trying to take in everything at once. The woman was holding my hand leading me into the house while the ocean was singing my name. As the waves went out they called "Kor..." and as they softly crashed against the rocks they said, "...ri". Sounds strange I know but that's what I heard.

"But you've seen nothing but the driveway. Come on in to see it all." The man who appeared to be a butler grinned at me. I don't know why I thought he was a butler, he had on golfing attire. Maybe it was his demeanor that led me to that thought. Or maybe it was my own daydreaming that made me to believe that I was in an overly large Villa for two with servants to heed our every call.

"Mom, dad, I want you all to meet the infamous Koriana Blackstone." I was in shock. Kevin had brought me home to meet his parents. We'd only been seeing each other for a few weeks but I guess if you would count the time before our two year breather, than it would probably add up to a years' time.

"Now why would you shock the girl like that Kevin, you should have warned her. Let's sit her down she looks as though she's going to pass out." They were all laughing at me but in a good way. The golfer, Kevin's dad, lead me to the patio near the massive pool while Kevin retrieved our bags from the car. I heard the round woman, his mom; say that she'll get some iced tea for me.

"First time in Charleston?" he asked me still grinning. Ernie, I was told later, was a retired Marine, who never looked back at Chicago after his tour of duty and never wanted to be more than five miles from the ocean. "I seem to lose my bearings if I can't smell the deep blue" he said chuckling. Interesting how a person would describe an old person as chuckling and a young person as laughing. Oh, sorry, that was just a quick thought.

"Yes it is sir."

"Sir...? Kevin, get this girl out of here!" Oh my Lord, I couldn't believe my ears. I was about to dive over the pool and into the ocean when the round woman came out with the iced tea.

"Ernie, you devil you. Leave the poor child alone" the round woman giggled sitting a tall glass of liquid on the stained glass table next to me. I grabbed the glass as if it supplied the very essence of life inside of it. I didn't realize how fast I was drinking until I saw Kevin's shoes through the bottom of it.

"What are you two doing to my woman?" Kevin sat in the chair next to me while his parents continued to grin down at me in amusement. I should have been offended but for some reason I began to enjoy their jester.

"They're adorable honey. They are simply adorable." I said finally able to smile.

"Lord, have mercy! Honey child you shouldn't have called this old man adorable."

"Clarice, hush your mouth girl, I'm finally getting attention from a younger woman, and don't you dare stop her." They all laughed again at something I found strange. Ernie was very handsome, from where I was sitting. I wouldn't be surprised if he didn't have a twenty year old college filly within his five mile limit. In fact, if I met him under other conditions... well, maybe not, but it's good to know how well Kevin was going to age. Even Clarice held on to a great amount of young beauty. She was plump in all the "love me good" areas, her skin was tight, hands were quick and steady and the twinkle in her eyes were giving the stars above a run for their money, or for their sparkle I should say.

"Pops are you trying to steal my woman? Do we have to go on the battle grounds for this?" Kevin stood toe to toe with his dad. They squared off in a playful manner, hugged and then headed inside.

"Watch the clock now, everyone will be here shortly" Clarice yelled after them. "Don't you worry dear; they're just going to shoot some pool." I guess I had a worried look on my face but it wasn't because of them. Clarice said "everyone will be here shortly". Who was everyone? And how short was "shortly". It was already going on eleven O'clock at night. Who visits this late? "Everyone dear" Clarice answered. Had I asked that out loud? Clarice went on to explain how the "Spade family, every year on this date; be it weekend or weekday, come here for mid-night, rum pancakes."

"Rum" It was my turn to be tickled. She said that all her sisters, Ernie's brothers and all the kids and wives and such, travel by plane, train, boats and automobiles for their family holiday. "You give it to the kids too?"

"Honey, yes but we put rum flavor in theirs. I remember one time I made a mistake and served Kevin rum pancakes from the adult batch..." she began to laugh. "He was giggling until the sun came up. It was funny for a moment but it made his stomach hurt for days. He'd caught on to some kind of spasm or something and couldn't stop laughing. Weird thing it was, never seen anything like it. Poor boy was crying tears and laughing at the same time."

"Wow! Is that why he doesn't drink?" I said suddenly concerned with his present state.

"I never thought about it Kori, maybe so. So now we feed the children first off so there'll be no mistakes." She laughed again as she grabbed my hand and guided me into the kitchen. "That actually works out better for us grown folks because the children play awhile, eat, bath and are dancing with the sand man by the time we're ready for the bond fire sing along." She stopped and looked down at my brand new Channel sandals 'click clacking' on the tiled floor. "It'd be good if you go into the first guest bedroom suite, second floor door on the left, and change into those slippers I bought you. Size nine correct?" How did she know and how long had she known that I was coming? Again, reading my mind she says "I spoke to Kevin while you were in the furniture store" and winked at me.

I never gave it too much thought as to whom Kevin was speaking with on the phone but I guess that explains his child like gestures that he was making with his feet as he spoke but all of this was crazy to me.

Flying to South Carolina on an impulse, like geese, high-end shopping for everything that I needed like celebrities and now, being spoiled in a huge beach house on the ocean.

I almost fell out when I opened the doors to our suite. Plush carpet, a king size four posted bed and drapery and quilts that Queen Victoria herself would adore, hit me like lightening, except the beauty hit me in a good way. The adjoining bathroom was half the size of the suite itself; with his and her commodes', double sinks on the vanity and a steam shower tucked in the corner. We even had a kitchenette stylishly positioned at the far right of the suite. I was certain the giddy feeling in my stomach would last a month or two. I ran and jumped on the bed like a little kid kicking and screaming in silence. I laid there staring at the ceiling wondering how I could stay there forever.

I couldn't think of anything at the moment so I rushed back downstairs to help out. There was lots of laughter and pan rattling as I entered the kitchen and just as I was wondering what kind of personalities to expect, a roar of "Kori's" rang out like a chorus. I smiled and laughed as ten family members hugged and asked me "what's a nice girl like you doing with a nice guy like Kevin?" I've never seen anything like this. Everyone was friendly not only with me but with each other. My family would have gone through five arguments by now, one being about who would be in the kitchen and two, who didn't contribute to the cause. Instead, the Spade family was chattering about, working in stations if you will, and taking turns monitoring the kids who were little angels in our presence.

Kevin finally emerged from the depths of battle, against his dad and uncles at the pool table, grinning at my floured hands and face I'd encountered having the time of my life with the women in the kitchen. After he left I found out that each woman had to take a shot of rum each time their mate entered the kitchen and I was the first to fall in line. I believe Kevin knew of this because for the next half hour he returned to the kitchen for a fork, then a napkin and then directions to the pool. All the ladies took a shot of rum with me on that one.

Even at one in the morning, the night felt young. The boats docked outside of their house seemed to rock to the music as everyone laughed and ate rum pancakes. Kevin and I sung a duet by Marvin Gaye and Tammy Terrell, for our bond fire song. We even received encore calls before everyone turned in for the night, or shall I say morning.

"Honey, do we have to go back?" I asked Kevin as the sun began to rise. We'd taken advantage of the poolside bed, and made love on it at least four times. I actually lost count but I knew that I would never lose any part of this memory.

"Yes baby. You do have a business to take over or even start up one of your own and this place will always be here for you." Kevin snuggled into my silence and sighed. "Ok fine. We can stay a week." I turned over and gave him a million kisses. This was going to be the best week ever.

JASON

Sitting here waiting on Kori to arrive has got me feeling uneasy, nervous in a way. I felt this way our prom night; I was getting my date something to drink when I heard someone call out her name. I turned in the direction of her reply just in time to see the most beautiful smile I have ever seen. When she walked in it was like I couldn't breathe, I didn't hear anything, see anything, but her... each step seemed to be in slow motion, taking an eternity for her to reach me as I waited eagerly in anticipation, while enjoying her every stride.

"Are you going to get my bags or what?" Kori, wearing that same smile as prom night, was standing at the passenger side of my car, catching me off guard. South Carolina must have been a good thing for her; her skin was glowing, she had a fresh hairdo and her smile was so bright that every man that passed stopped and took a deep breath in her honor.

I jumped out the car to grab her bags and hoped that she wasn't paying too much attention to me because while she was basking in the glow of love, I was here catching hell. I'd lost my job due to down-sizing, Sharon was still singing the blues and I had to make some quick decisions about my living situation. My Landlord was not a patient woman and staying with Sharon was so way out of the question, NASA couldn't see it.

"You look like hell." Kori giggled as she hugged me. I felt like hell until I felt the warmth of her body. A scent of vanilla tickled my nose as she pulled away to look at me. "Dang Jay, what's going on?" She had frown lines in her forehead now and I hate that I put them there.

"I'm cool, get in the car before I get a ticket." Kori didn't move and I knew she wasn't until I said something more convincing. "Please get in. I'll tell you as soon as we pull off."

She hesitated, then handed me a small carry on piece of luggage. Kori sat with her arms crossed watching the side of my face until I pulled onto a main street.

"Spill it." Kori, with her motherly attitude, just shook her head and made a few moans and grumbles as I described my week to her. I can feel her thoughts leading to confronting Sharon and slapping me a few times for putting up with such nonsense. "So she wants you to continue getting her nails and stuff done with your savings and she can't even cook you a decent meal." She shook her head. "You know this is your fault don't you?"

"How is it my fault?"

"If you had paced yourself with her like I said, you wouldn't be going through this. A woman gets a decent man and don't know how to treat him. That woman makes me sick to my stomach." Kori sucked air through her teeth. I was afraid to tell her the rest but I had no choice. I told her that Sharon was pregnant and that I was the father. I felt Kori's heart stop as she pulled up her calendar on her cell phone. She then sat quietly for a few blocks, let out some air and looked out the window next to her. "When did you stop using condoms?" I told her that I've always used them until that day at the café. I wanted to tell her that I was so mixed up about what I was feeling for her and Sharon was going on and on about how good Kevin looked, that I took Sharon home to screw her brains out so she'd forget about Kevin and so that I could forget about her. But I only told Kori that I was horny.

"So you think she's pregnant after one week?"

"Yeah" I said feeling stupid. By the way she put it, it did sound impossible.

"And you think she's pregnant by you?" What did she mean, by "you"?

"Who else..." I stopped. I did not want to hear another word. If Sharon was pregnant, then yes, it was possible that it wasn't by me. Most of the time, I hate it when Kori is right and this is one of those times. What the hell was Sharon thinking? Sleep with another dude, leave me stranded for two weeks so I can be all horny for her and not use a condom. That's why she was so pissed that day and my dumb ass fell for it getting jealous for nothing. Come to think of it, she probably did that on purpose too.

"That's why I said…"

"Please don't." I cut Kori off. I knew exactly what she was going to say and I didn't want to hear it. Surprisingly, Kori respected my wishes and sat quietly until we arrived at her apartment building.

"You want to hide out with me for a few days? Kevin had to go to L.A. so I could use a little company." Kori gave me a girlish smirk and then pouted her lips. She was so cute right now she made me smile. I'd probably ruin our friendship if I stayed with her, feeling like I do. "Ok, fine, I'll keep my cozy sofa to myself. Can you at least hang around and have dinner with me?"

"That, I can do." I kissed her hand and drove around the corner to her favorite restaurant and she smiled her approval. It's amazing how we know each other so well that mere looks can tell us what each other want. That's all I want in a relationship is for someone to know me and love me any damn way. All of this bending and stretching on my part is wearing me down. Sharon wants me to be a successful artist but wants me to spend every waking moment with her. She wants me to save money but yet buy her everything that she desire.

Why can't she be like Kori and just let me be? We've eaten dinner, dessert and we talked in the car in front of her building for an hour and not once has she looked at her phone or called Kevin. I, on the other hand, have felt my phone vibrate nonstop for the last two hours. After Sharon and I had sex last week she's been too busy to talk, and now since I told her that I was picking Kori up from the airport, I seem to be her main priority.

"Can you take me to the doctor tomorrow?" Kori pulled me from my thoughts. "I really don't feel like calling a taxi in the morning."

"How early do I need to be here?" I don't know why this woman won't buy a car.

"Seven." She said it like she was squeezing the word from a tube. She could have said three in the morning and I would have been here at two. "As a matter of fact, why don't you just sleep on the sofa, test it out and then you'll already be here in the morning." Kori Jumped out of my car like there was no need for further discussion. Once we got into her apartment, Kori handed me some towels, a pillow, a sheet and a blanket. She then went into her bedroom closet and found a pair of basketball shorts that I left here before and a t-shirt.

"We'll have popcorn and a movie, my room, in twenty minutes." Kori turned to leave then stopped. "And that was not a question." She smiled and disappeared into her room. Her room; why was I so nervous about that? I've been in there plenty of times. I've even slept in her bed a few tired nights. In the words of my nephew, "What to do? What to do? What to do do do."

KORI

Oh my god! I am locked in my own bathroom standing in the tub. What answer do you want first? Why am I standing in my tub? Or why am I locked in my bathroom? Well I locked myself in my bathroom because I just felt Jason get an erection for me. At least I think it was for me. You see, we fell asleep watching... awe man I can't think of the name of it... but it was a movie, I'll just leave it at that. And normally when Jason sleeps in my bed, he stays to one side and I stay to the other but tonight, when I woke up, Jason was right behind me, with an erection.

At first I thought that maybe he was dreaming or something but then he said my name. I jumped out of that bed so fast and ran into the bathroom. I don't know rather to be disgusted or flattered. No matter how comfortable I've been with Jason, I've never ever thought of him that way. And that's why I'm standing in my tub, not because of my feelings but because I don't want Jason to hear me pacing. He's been through so much and if he's actually awake and know that I felt him, it could be humiliating. So do I pretend nothing happened and that I just had to use the bathroom or do I just come right out and ask him about it? You're right, I'll pretend nothing happened. Maybe he was dreaming... about me... this is crazy. I'll just call Kevin to get my mind off of it.

"Hello." A groggy, woman's voice answered on the first ring. I hung up the phone and checked the number. Ok, I didn't press the wrong number so I dialed it out instead just to be sure.

"Hello." The same voice said more sternly.

"Yes, who is this?"

"Honey, who are you? You called my man's phone." I just stood stunned just for a second. I've never been one to argue over a man but damn, hadn't I just met his whole family. I was about to say some choice words when I heard Kevin in the background laughing and telling whomever the woman was not to answer his phone again. He grabbed the phone from her.

"Kori, baby is that you?" I didn't say a word. Kevin called out my name again but this time without the humor. I still didn't say a word. I hung up the phone and sat on the toilet trying to make since of it all. My phone rung, I pressed the "ignore" button. It rung again, I silenced it and turned it off. I looked at the clock; it was two thirty in the morning. I needed to run so I went back into my bedroom and put on some running gear. I was so discombobulated; I'd forgotten Jason was even there let alone in my bedroom. I looked over at him and saw that he was turned towards the wall.

"Jay. Jay!" I called out to him. I really didn't want to wake him but I seriously couldn't go out there alone.

"What's wrong baby?" Lord why is he calling me baby? I can't deal with that right now.

"Please get up and run with me."

"Why so early?" Jason turned over and looked at me. I guess that he could see the pain or the confusion on my face because he didn't ask any more questions. He quickly got out of the bed, went to the living room, put on his gym shoes and his jacket. He came back into my bedroom where I was still leaning against the wall, grabbed my hand and lead me out the door.

JASON

I don't know why Kori is upset but I was silently praying, as we ran along the beach, that it wasn't because of me. I was dreaming about her and for some reason, I smelled her in my sleep. I woke up when I felt her jump out of the bed and then I felt my hard on. I wanted to run up out of there. I was going to apologize when she came out of the bathroom but by that time, embarrassment had set in and I all I wanted to do was to go and hide. I thought about going out to the sofa but I thought that would be too obvious so I just tried to seep into the wall until she called my name.

We've been running hard for thirty minutes now, without a word. I was in my thoughts and she was definitely in hers. Kori began to slow down, and then she began to pace in a circle. I just followed her lead.

"A woman answered Kevin's phone." She said between pants. I was so relieved and pissed at the same time. I was about to say something but Kori kept talking. "I didn't even know what to say. Then he got on the phone laughing as if it was a big joke." I sat down in the wet grass and watched her circle a pile of ants breaking down a slice of tomato on the ground. "I'm trying to make some since of it but I can't. I'm thinking maybe there was some kind of party and he laid his phone down but then there wasn't any party noise in the background and the woman sounded as if she just woke up."

"Maybe she was a smoker." I tried to make her laugh.

"Jay, she just woke up. Even if she was a smoker, shouldn't he have been more upset that she answered his phone?"

"I guess, depends on the setting." Kori stopped abruptly and looked at me.

"Really, Jason? So what kind of setting is it ok for a woman, other than me to answer your phone?" She had a point. Bastard doesn't know how well he has it. Kori is perfect; beautiful, smart, sexy and she has much business sense. You can't find all of that in one woman these days. "Are you listening Jason?" I spaced out and missed something.

"I'm sorry, what did you say?" Kori hate to feel ignored and I hate to make her feel that way. She just puffed out some air and repeated herself.

"Would you lie your phone down at a party?" Kori stood in front of me looking tired. She looked tired of games and tricks from men, tired of dishonesty. I told her no. I could have tried to defend Kevin just because he was a man but Kori was important to me and I just couldn't do it. I stood up and the morning wind from the lake instantly hit the wet spot on the back of my shorts. I wrapped my arms around her. She was hesitant at first but then she cradled into my arms and softly cried. Knowing Kori, her tears were merely for allowing herself to trust again and not so much for what Kevin did. We stood there in silence for a moment and then I could feel her wiping her nose with my jacket.

"So that's how you feel about me?" I laughed.

"You wouldn't want me to use my own jacket now would you? Besides, you owe me after what you did this morning."

"I didn't do..." She got me. Kori was now calling me out on my physical mishap. I laughed it off with her but I wasn't sure I liked the fact that it didn't make her think twice about me. I guess what's meant to be will be and if Kori and I remain the same, this will forever be the best relationship I've ever had.

"Oh don't flatter yourself; I just had to pee that's all.

"Yeah, whatever" She laughed and we raced back to her place.

KORI

Ok, well, my phone is still in the off position so I have yet to talk with Kevin. I am so not ready for that. I need to clear my head of fantasies and my soul of emotions so I can still come out on my "independent top". I should have known better anyway, I did know better and still got caught up. Anyway, Jason and I got back to my apartment, showered, dressed and then we went out to have an early breakfast. Now he's gone and I'm sitting in this clinic waiting on my test results. I hate the triage service but the nurses inside are great. Jason call it the chop shop, which it is, but my girl Shaniqua works here and I get free HIV tests every six months; I never want to be caught off guard.

"Kori" my girl was calling me in a whisper. I walked over to the door that led to the back, at which she was standing. Shaniqua had an amusing look on her face so I knew that she was about to dish out some gossip. She began to lead me down a hall towards a recovery room.

"So when you're done with your urine test, just come back down this hall to get back to the waiting room." I was about to ask her what the heck she was talking about but then I noticed some other nurses heading our way. Shaniqua handed me a urine sample cup, the girl is always prepared. After her co-workers passed by, we stopped in front of one of the recovery rooms, looked over our shoulders for clearance, and Shaniqua softly pushed me forward and motioned for me to pull the curtain back at one of the stalls. I did, and I almost hit the floor when I saw Sharon resting, in the abortion recovery room. Shaniqua had to run in and stop me from dragging her ass out of that bed. One more inch and I would have held tight to that perfectly manicured toe of hers. Jason talks a lot of smack but he loved this girl and now I have to tell him that she threw away his child.

Either the air outside was muggy or my head was cloudy, either way, I couldn't breathe. I'd walked for thirty minutes before realizing that I was walking in the wrong direction. I needed to talk to Jason, but what was I going to say and how was I going to say it. I stood in the middle of the sidewalk just thinking; what if he didn't believe me, should I ask Shaniqua for a copy of Sharon's discharge papers? No because Sharon can sue the clinic, Shaniqua will get fired and then she'd kill Sharon and I'd be putting money on Shaniqua's commissary books for the rest of her life and I'd be stuck raising her five kids. I definitely needed another route.

The vibration from my phone pulled me out of my trance, I didn't even remember turning it on. Kevin was ringing my phone and I seemed to have missed twenty calls from him since last night and I was about to miss this one too. I didn't have the mindset to "hear him out" at this moment. I gathered my senses, ran into the drug store for a few items, held a cab to Jason's house, pulled up my big girl panties and rang the doorbell. Jason opened the door looking a bit strange but the wider he opened the door the more I understood. Sharon had her feet up on the sofa with a blanket across her legs, reading a magazine with one hand and sipping from a mug with another. There were moving boxes everywhere and the remains of Chinese food sprawled out on the coffee table near a few baby magazines, meaning Sharon didn't tell Jason the good news.

"We need to talk" I said to Jason ignoring the pasted on smile Sharon gave me.

"Hi Kori, I'm so glad you're here." Sharon was attempting to get off the sofa but Jason rushed to her side and begged her not to move.

"Sharon fell down a couple of steps this morning and she insists on not resting." Jason said to me but he didn't take his eyes off of Sharon.

"I'm fine Jason, you're making me nauseous. Girl, men act like women can't handle a little thing like falling." Sharon looked to me for support, I almost screamed. "I showed him the ultra sound photo and he hasn't stopped pampering me yet." Ok, I can't take anymore of this; Jason was beginning to rub her feet now.

"So you're pregnant?" they both looked at me in surprise.

"Yes, I thought Jason would have told you by now." Sharon was now looking at Jason in surprise.

"Kori I told you."

"Yes but I thought that from this morning's events that you'd be singing a different song by now." There it was. The truth was out there in the open air, suspended by shocking gasp of breath. Sharon jumped up so fast she almost knocked over the table leaving Jason's hands empty and wondering where her feet went. "Funny thing though, I wouldn't have guessed that an ultra sound photo would be a suitable parting gift."

"What are you talking about Kori?" Jason was still sitting; probably afraid he'd fall over had he stood up.

"Nothing baby, she's saying absolutely nothing. And even if she was saying something, it would probably sound like the ramblings of a jealous woman." Sharon picked the blanket up from the floor, moved the coffee table forward and up righted a water bottle all while looking me straight in the eye.

"I don't know why you're looking at me like that Sharon, because the way I feel right now, I can kick your tail all the way to the trash can you left Jason's baby in." I almost forgot that Jason was in the room until I heard the table falling over. He'd finally found the nerve to move and when he did; he jumped across the table, his foot nabbed the edge of it and tipped it over. He almost crashed into me trying to keep Sharon from hitting me. "Let her go Jason, please let her go."

"Just because Kevin dumped you doesn't give you the right to come in here and tell lies on me." Sharon was now bent over holding her stomach, playing on Jason's sensitive side no doubt.

"What do you mean Kevin dumped me?" I looked at Jason and saw something that I thought I'd never see across his face, guilt. "You talked to her about me and Kevin?" My face felt hot and my left eye was beginning to twitch, which meant tears were soon to follow.

"I wasn't trying to... it just slipped out Kori" Jason was stammering.

"You don't have to explain anything to her when she's trying to tear us apart. She's just mad because I'm moving in with you and we're about to have the baby she's always wanted." Sharon was back in her position on the sofa and Jason was just standing there looking stupid.

"What? Where do you receive your information? You sound like a mad woman." I laughed to keep from crying, literally. "Jason you're not going to say anything?"

"Honestly I have no idea what you two are talking about."

"I saw her at the clinic this morning Jason. Sharon's aborted your baby!" I yelled. I couldn't believe I had to actually say the words. What was wrong with Jason? It was like he was walking around with a cloud on top of his head. He slowly turned and looked at Sharon.

"Baby I think it's time that you put her out." Sharon said.

"He's not going to put me out." I said.

"Maybe you should leave." He said.

Well, damn! Another first, Jason was putting me out of his apartment. I stand corrected; his and Sharon's apartment. When did all of this happen? Did he talk to her while I was in the shower this morning or had he planned to move her in already and didn't tell me about it. We were all silent for a moment, thinking, planning our next lines or our next moves. I looked at the two of them and couldn't help but to feel pity. Sharon had reopened her magazine as if nothing happened and Jason... Jason looked like life had just been sucked right out of him. He needed a moment to sort things out in his head and Sharon and I arguing was not going to help him so yes, it was best that I left.

I reached in my purse and handed Jason one of the items that I picked up from the store. He looked down at the pregnancy test and stumbled backwards into a chair. I don't know if he was relieved that he didn't have to think of his next move or overwhelmed by the task at hand. Once I got outside, I said a silent prayer for Sharon and pressed the necessary buttons on my phone to return Kevin's call. Now was absolutely a perfect time to discuss our future or lack thereof, and I wanted my dog. And after we're done, I'm turning my phone off again for at least two days.

JASON

"Was the baby mine?"

"What difference does it makes? We can get past all of this." Sharon was crying and slobbering all over me. In the hour since Kori left, we've been arguing back and forward about her taking the pregnancy test. First she argued that she didn't have to pee, and then that it had to be the first urine of the morning and then she tried to threaten to leave me if I took Kori's word over hers. After I told her to leave, she agreed to take the test but then we argued again when I told her that I wanted to see her pee on the stick.

"Was the baby mine?" I yelled, Sharon grew silent and at that moment I knew my question didn't need an answer. Shaking my head at my damn self and hating her for her selfishness and at me, again for giving her try after try, forgiving and forgetting, probably missed out on a better opportunity with Kori. Why have I wasted my time with this girl, or any other female for that matter? None of them measured up to Kori. When did I start doing that? Why am I measuring women against Kori? We're just friends right?

"No the baby wasn't yours." Sharon was saying, but my head was whirling around the thoughts of Kori. "I wouldn't dare have a child with you. Ha! I can't believe I lowered my standards to be with you."

"And I guess your baby daddy lowered his standards to be with you." I can't believe she's trying to make me feel bad about her lies. I don't care what she says, I'm a good man.

"Don't worry about him; you need to worry about what you're lacking."

"Lacking?"

"You lack motivation, determination and..."

"I must have something because you're still here!" I yelled. Sharon grabbed her things and rushed out of the door. A deep feeling of relief came over me as she started her car and drove off. I don't know if it was because I was finally being rid of her or that I didn't have to co-parent with someone as narrow minded as she.

I suddenly had the urge to talk to Kori; I dialed her phone number several times but it kept going to her voice mail. I had to tell her that I thought she was "the one" for me so I grabbed my jacket and rush out the door, but remembering that my keys were on the table, I tried to stop the door from closing, to no avail, almost slamming my finger in the process. I held a cab but ended up walking part of the way because my credit card was missing and I only had twenty dollars in cash. I didn't let that stop me, I was determined to see Kori that night and as I walked those last eight blocks in the cold rain, I prayed that she would be home because she had yet to answer her phone.

Just as I was thinking that the night couldn't get any worse, the rain got heavier, the wind blew harder, my shoes and socks were soaked and the doorman was reluctant to let me inside the building. When Kori opened her door, I was so relieved that I grabbed her up into a hug and squeezed her until she yelled at me to let her go. The speech I prepared in my mind was now null and void. I couldn't let her go completely though, it was like I hadn't seen her in years so I began to kiss her all over her face. I kissed her forehead, her cheeks, her nose and then her mouth. And then I kissed her mouth again but longer this time. I thought I felt our souls meeting for the first time, heat was rising and... I stopped. I looked at Kori and she was staring at me blankly.

"What are you doing Jason?" Kori asked me. I was confused, wasn't she just returning my kiss? Wasn't her soul greeting mine or was my eagerness fooling me?

"I want you Kori" I said bluntly. She should know this by now.

"You want me how?"

"You know how Kori, please don't deny me, not tonight." I was begging but I couldn't turn it off. I tried to pull her towards me and she pushed me away. Her hands felt like cold steal, a harshness that was unbearable. I stepped away from her. "You don't feel this?"

"No Jay, I don't. We're friends and I don't want to change that."

"Just friends?" I asked but I knew in my mind that she was right, but my emotions were defining it differently. "Is it because of Kevin because I can treat you way better than he can? All he knows how to do is spend money but no one can love you better than I can Kori."

"You're right, no one can and that is the one thing I don't want to change about us Jason." Kori was being unreasonable. What's better than a relationship with your best friend?

"I know that you're probable scared or maybe you don't want to hurt Kevin's feelings but to hell with him. If he wanted you the way that I do right now, then he would be here and not somewhere else having females answering his phone." I was getting pissed. Why do women overlook the "good man" in front of them to give time to the asshole standing behind him? I guess that I'm guilty of doing the same thing by overlooking Kori all these years but when you know better you do better.

"Did you hear what you just said?" She didn't let me answer. "You said the way you want me right now. Jason you're just hurt because of Sharon and you just probably need someone to comfort you but I'm not that woman."

"I don't need someone, I need you Kori. And what Sharon has done has nothing to do with this moment right here." Kori was now crying and I hated myself for making it happen but I needed to say these words. Kori turned from me and walked over to her window, excusing me from her presence. She didn't ask me to leave but she didn't have to, enough was said tonight to last an eternity; I loved Kori and she loved me, but the timing was off. I softly closed the door behind me and began my journey home.

PRESENT DAY

As Kori pressed the buttons on the vending machine, she couldn't help but to think about how she and Jason got to this point. When Jason left her apartment that tragic night, her world began to change, drastically. She couldn't truthfully say that she had never thought of her and Jason in a manner of which he was speaking, but it was little stuff like; if I had a man to do this like Jason or who understood her like Jason. Who wouldn't want a physical relationship with someone who knew them in and out, their likes and dislikes and who knew when to just shut up so you could vent out the things that were bothering you about them. Kori's mind never went completely there until she heard Jason say the words himself. However if she was to be totally honest with herself, she would be able to admit that there were times she'd wished their hugs lasted a little longer or the sweet peck on the lips that he always gave her, was pressed just a little bit harder against hers.

After coming to the realization that she owed it to the both of them to at least complete their conversation, Kori ran to her room, threw on a sweat suit and gym shoes, grabbed her purse and keys and ran head on into Kevin who was approaching her door. She'd bumped him so hard it made her bounce off of him and it would have made her hit her own door, had he not grabbed hold of her. Kori then made a mental note to speak very harshly with the doorman as soon as she laid eyes on him; letting Jason in was cool but he didn't know Kevin well enough to just let him come up to her apartment.

"Ouch, you're in a hurry." Kevin said smiling down at Kori as if he hadn't missed a beat.

"Oh sorry, I'm in a hurry." Kori turned to lock her door and proceeded to the elevator.

"You really are in a hurry. Can I come in for a minute?"

"What do you want Kevin, I thought we settled everything over the phone?" Kori was irritated by his unexpected visit considering the fact that he initially didn't have much time to talk over the phone a few hours ago let alone a visit. She was now on a mission and Kevin was in her way.

"Well I wanted to explain myself a little further."

"There's no need for all of that. You're a sports agent; who from time to time hire women to reel your clients in, throw parties and sometimes get caught up in the action. I got all of that over the phone." Kori now hated the fact that she gave Kevin even just a little bit of her time. He's always been too busy for her and she didn't know what made her think that this time would be different.

"Well it's a little more to it Kori. Ralentir je suisen train de vousparler." Kevin raised his voice a bit as Kori bounded for the lobby doors when they reached the first floor. Kevin's French was sexy, when spoken at the right moment and this was not that moment. "Slow down!"

"I can't slow down; I'm trying to find Jason. Something is wrong with him." Kori didn't want to go into the truth with Kevin at this point because men have a crazy way of thinking when they're being dumped; they could have beaten you, spit on you and cheated on you but they'll never believe those are the reasons that you are leaving them. In their minds, it's always because of another man.

"Why don't you just call him?"

"I tried that, but it's going straight to his voicemail. Can you give me a ride?" Kori wished that she had bit her tongue before asking Kevin to help her. And by the look on Kevin's face, he wished she had too.

"You won't even stand here and have a conversation with me but you want me to drive you around to find some other man? Unbelievable."

"He's not just some other man, he's my..." Kori stopped herself from saying friend. Jason was not just her friend, he was her everything and nothing was ever going to change that. "You're right Kevin, thank you for your time."

"That's it right there."

"What?"

"Jason is the reason that I could never get a fight out of you." Kevin was shaking his head at her looking like he just solved the cure to athlete's feet or something.

"Now why would I try to fight you Kevin?"

"Exactly! People... couples who care about each other fight and argue over their disappointments in each other or their disagreements. You've never shown me any of that because you've always had Jason, your friend, to run back to so whatever I did didn't upset you enough to even complain about it." Kevin sat down on the lobby sofa looking exhausted. He held his head in his hands for a moment and then exhaled loudly. "You know sometimes I would not call you for days just to see if you'd fuss at me but you didn't even give me an angry tone when I would finally call" he laughed. "I used to think that you just weren't that type of woman, but now, seeing how anxious you look to get out of here to find Jason, I know the truth; Jason has always been your man."

"I've never slept with Jason. He and I are just..."

"Friends, yes I hear what you're saying but your actions says differently." Kevin stood up and walked towards Kori who tried to brace herself for whatever was to come next. What Kevin was saying was speaking volumes, a truth that she hadn't realized. "He's your date for family functions, friendly gatherings, dinner, and movies and when you need a little something more on the physical side then that's when you prey on little brothers such as me. And when you get tired of the charade... well that's when you find something so terribly wrong with us that 'it just isn't going to work out' and leave us thinking that we were the problem."

Kori stepped back and looked at Kevin for a moment. He was so right about everything that she couldn't do anything but smile at him. Her smile then became a wide grin and then she began to laugh uncontrollably. Kevin was starting to look angry but then he began to smile with realization that he had helped her and with the relief that he wasn't such a bad guy after all.

Kori quickly turned from Kevin, ran out to the street and held a cab. Kevin was still standing in her lobby when the cab pulled off, heading towards Lake Shore Drive for the longest but most exhilarating ride ever to Jason's apartment.

"Your stuff is at the bottom ma'am" a young lady was pointing at the box of Mike & Ike's at the bottom of the vending machine, yanking Kori from her thoughts. She wondered if Sharon had made it there yet and suddenly wished that she'd gotten dressed before leaving Jason's room, the people in the lobby were starting to stare at her robe and pajamas. When Kori returned to Jason's room, Jason was standing at the foot of his bed, packing his bag. His I.V. was removed and the oxygen cords were on his bed tray. There was no sign of Sharon or of her being there and Kori dared not to ask.

"You're packing already? How long was I gone?" She laughed.

"You were gone long enough for my last vital check, the reading of my blood test results and discharge instructions." Jason smiled looking healthier by the minute. She never did find him the night she went looking for him. When he didn't answer the door, Kori used her spare key to get into the apartment only to find him gone. His keys were on the table so she thought that maybe he just stepped out to get something to eat so she waited. Waiting turned into dozing off and dozing off turned into snoring. Kori was jilted awake by the ringing of her cell phone the next morning, with a nurse on the other end telling her that Jason was in the hospital with Pneumonia, not the tragic kind, she also explained.

Apparently he realized, after being soaked by the freezing rain, that he couldn't possibly walk all the way home to the south side, then he managed to get on the train without a fare, which was blowing cold air and he instantly got a fever. The fever made him drift off to sleep and some kind citizen thought that he was dead and notified the train operator, who panicked and called for medical attention. He woke up just before the paramedic arrived but since he was feeling so bad, he allowed them to take him to the hospital and gave Kori's name as next to kin.

"Awesome, Let me pack my little bag and let's hit the road jack." Kori grabbed her bag from the closet and began to change into a pair of jeans under her gown.

"Sharon only brought me a few things that I left at her house and a set of keys that I can no longer use. She said that it was a pad lock and a bright orange sticker on my apartment door." Kori didn't respond but Jason knew that she was secretly scanning the room for a bag or box that wasn't there before, just as he knew she was worried about Sharon's visit in the first place. Kori had run out so fast that he didn't get a chance to explain it to her. Her instant attitude made him smile because he knew that it meant she cared about him.

"I guess you can stay at my place until you get better and we figure out your living situation." Kori only excuse for the giddiness inside her was that Sharon was out of Jason's life and she was going to make sure that it was for good. The two of them rode in silence with their personal thoughts of what's to come next. Jason was praying that he'd be able to behave like a gentleman during his stay and not like the horny boy he portrayed a few weeks ago. He really appreciated Kori and he was glad that his confession didn't turn her away from him. Kori on the other hand was suppressing her excitement of all the possibilities of what can transpire between the two of them. 'Go slow' Kori had to remind herself, as she helped Jason out of the car in front of her building. The doorman, who was very apologetic after Kori gave him a few choice words, ran out and insisted on parking Jason's car and bringing the bags up for them when he was done.

Jason was so engrossed in his story about Sharon's visit that he hadn't noticed that Kori had stopped walking down the corridor to her apartment. "What's wrong, why did you stop right there?"

"I live here, where are you going?" Kori smiled.

"Oh so that's what you were doing last week when I heard you say something about moving guys." Kori didn't respond, she just opened the door to her new apartment and stepped aside so that Jason can enter first. "So is this place bigger, smaller or does it has that balcony you always wanted?"

"It's bigger and it has a balcony but that's not why I wanted it" Kori said ushering Jason towards a closed door.

"Spare me the suspense why don't you..." Jason's words caught in his throat along with the emotions that were now trying to flood over them. Kori opened the door to a bedroom that had all of his personal belongings in it. His bed, his dresser, his basketball and even the things that he had on his wall at his old apartment was now in this bedroom. He was afraid to turn to look at her because he knew that she was also gushing with emotions and he hated to see her cry. Kori followed Jason into the room and watched him take inventory of all his things; his silence was all she needed to verify that she had done a good thing.

"I wasn't sure what to do with all your stuff so I put everything except your art kits and easel into storage for you. Whenever you get a job you're going to owe me big time." Kori said knowing that having him there with her was payback and more. Kori made sandwiches and warmed some soup that they ate watching the evening news in the kitchen. Jason thanked her so many times that Kori threatened to kick him out if he said it once more. Kori washed the few dishes that they used while Jason took his evening dosage of medicine and made a few calls to let others know where to find him. Everything felt so natural to the both of them up to this point, it was bed time and awkwardness was setting in. Someone had to say something.

"I could..."

"Movie and popcorn in twenty minutes." Kori was always on point Jason thought. "I'm sorry what were you going to say Jason?" Jason shook his head because he actually forgot what he was going to say.

"Are we meeting in my room or yours?"

"Oh that's easy. I haven't had time to set my room up yet, I'd planned on sleeping on the sofa." They laughed and departed to change into their sleepwear. It took Kori a little longer because almost everything that she owned was see through and she wasn't trying to make that kind of statement just yet. She settled on a pair of boxing shorts and a t-shirt that he'd given her a long time ago for Christmas.

"Awe don't you look cute?" Jason teased as Kori crawled into bed. The television was on but the audio was muted. "I figured I'd tell you a bed time story first if you don't mind." Jason wrapped his arms around Kori as she snuggled into him. Nothing can be better than this they both thought.

"The one about how we met?" Kori asked.

"Would any other story be appropriate?" Jason tugged at her hair.

"Not at all" Kori said turning to face him. They looked at each other for a long moment and then Jason kissed Kori's forehead, her nose and then her lips. "I love you Jason."

"Girl I know that already now hush and let me tell my story." They laughed and stared into each other's eyes as they took turns telling their version of how they met. Although there will always be two sides to that story, there will only be one version of how they talked until the sun came up, how they laughed until they could hardly breathe and how they fell in love with one another on that night. Amazing how a man and woman can be so compatible, so understanding of one another and true love can still be ignored. If the two of them would have never opened their eyes and released their fears, they would have sadly remained just friends.

THE END

LOST AND FOUND

Lost and Found   Preface

Crosby thought about the definition of pride; *a becoming or dignified sense of what is due to oneself or one's position or character.* Hadn't he had some pride due to him? Wasn't he the one faithful these past two years? Who was she to tell him what he could get over, determining his worth? Crosby slammed his fist to the steering wheel spilling his coffee as he turned the corner to the crime scene. "Shit!" He mentally bit his tongue. Crosby once prided himself for being the only cop on the force that didn't use profanity but due to recent events with his fiancé, he have to learn to say "ex" in front of that, he'd gotten re-acquainted with four lettered curse words like an old friend.

Determined to get the coffee stain out of his pants leg, detective Crosby rubbed the brown spot vigorously with his tie. He refused to walk on the scene looking like an idiot. He knew all eyes would be on him, just waiting on him to... to look like a fool. This was his second major case, his second chance to gain some respect in the department.

Detective Crosby decided that the stain had won. So he tossed his tie in the back seat, grabbed his pen and pad and tucked his pride into his back pocket. His past was his and his alone; no one could change it but solving the case at hand, could make everyone else forget.

The scene wasn't what he'd expected; nothing in the apartment seemed to be out of place. The tossed pillows were neatly placed on the sofa, crystal ornaments were dancing on the end tables and there wasn't a speck of dust in the air. From what he could see of the kitchen, only a wine bottle and some glasses were on the counter. The victim either had company before the attack or she was expecting some. There were no visible prints on the glasses, but he made a mental note to have forensic bag them up with the bottle of wine for a closer look at the lab.

"Crosby, my man, how's it hanging?" Crosby hated how rookie cops pretended to know him. The rookie looked at the spot on his pants but dared not say anything.

"How're you doing officer? Has anyone else been in the room?" Crosby asked while quickly scanning the bedroom. There was no gun, no knife or any visible trail of blood. The body of a young lady was lying on the floor next to the bed. Her purse was turned over onto the bed next to a black silk dress, red bottom high heels and an invitation of some sort.

"Where might you be?" Crosby questioned the man in the photo above the bed. Such arrogance he thought. Why wasn't the wife in the picture? The bedroom was richly decorated with things Crosby couldn't afford. Channel bedspreads and curtains, carpet from the Imperial Garden Company and designer lamps were on the table. Crosby knew the brands due to his ex-fiancé drilling him on the finer things in life; information he'd never thought he'd use. Guess she was good for something he thought with a chuckle.

"No Crosby, you're the first one in" he nodded at his partner. "I guess that's good for something, huh." The rookie officers smile diminished as Crosby continued to study the room. The rookie cleared his throat and pulled out his note pad. "We have a twenty seven year old female, one Diane Crawford, husband, Thomas Crawford of D&T Financing. We arrived ten minutes ago. Initial call from a neighbor..." He turned the pages of his note book. "...um ...no name was given. And that's all we have detective." The rookie finished feeling proud.

"Oh, and there was no sign of a forced entry." His partner added, not wanting to be left out.

"Has the body been moved?" Crosby asked kneeling towards the victim. The blood on the left of the body looked smeared; as if she was pushed aside. Crosby examined her hands which were still balled into a fist, clutching a watch. Her lips were pouty and her eyebrows seemed to be frowning. "You sure she hasn't been moved" he turned to ask the rookie and in that same instant the victim grabbed him by the arm.

"Don't leave me here!" The victim screamed then passed out.

"What the...?" Crosby's heart was racing as he grabbed her arm and checked her pulse. He reached for his cell phone to call for paramedics. He looked around the room at the shocked rookies and just shook his head. They never checked her vitals but pronounced her dead upon their arrival. He looked down at the woman whose frown was now gone; her hands were at rest and she now seemed to be sleeping. I will find your attacker he thought, but more of a promise to himself then to the woman lying on the floor. Yes he was concerned about her but he needed this victory, this redemption from past failures; over looked clues, lazy investigations, cocky interrogations and just plain old ignorance. He dismissed the other officers, pulled on a pair of rubber gloves and began what became a two-hour thorough search for clues.

Diane tossed and turned, kicking Thomas several times before awakening with a jolt. She sat up breathing as if she'd been running from someone and large beads of sweat ran down her neck to confirm her urgency to get away. Her heart was pounding in her ears like an Ethiopians tribal war call. She could feel its pulse breathing off the walls, throbbing inside her soul. "The lord is my shepherd, the lord is my shepherd" she whispered over and over with her eyes closed until the music began to fade in her chest.

The room was dark with a hint of blue light at the top of the curtains, letting Diane know that it was early morning. She looked over at the bathroom and noted, again, that Thomas didn't leave the light on per her request. He knew the light soothed her at times like these but continued to argue about the light bill, in which she doubted very seriously, he even had an ounce of concern.

When she first came home, Thomas was very attentive and caring. He'd leave the bathroom light on and the door cracked open. When Diane would wake from her dreams he'd pour her a glass of water, rub her back until her breathing was normal and then listen to her explain the dream as if he was hearing it for the first time. She looked over at Thomas to see if she had awakened him. She hadn't, but Diane was unsure of how she felt about that.

Diane had been having these dreams since she woke up in the hospital three months ago. She'd dream that she was eating a plate of lobster and shrimp at a small table in the middle of a field of rocks. The moon was shining down on her like a spotlight but the sun was out also, shining in a different direction, as if life was going on somewhere without her. Then all of a sudden a man, whose face she couldn't see, appears at the other end of the table; pounding his fist and yelling over and over "I should have killed you". He would jump up to grab her but Diane would run towards the sun. She could feel the sun rays falling down on her skin like raindrops as she got closer but just before she could step into the light, the man would pull her by the hair and Diane would wake up screaming.

Knowing she wasn't going to fall back to sleep, Diane thought some fresh air would do her some good. She swung her legs over the edge of the bed and sunk her feet into the carpet. This, somehow, gave her comfort. It was soft, deep, and something stable that she didn't have to remember to "do" anything with. She had to learn that her clothes were on the left side of the dresser, shirts were to be hung, and shoes weren't allowed on the closet floor. Every pair of shoes had a perfect little slot and every pair of pants were either hung on its labeled hanger or folded onto a perspective shelf. Diane didn't know if these were Thomas's rules or hers but she couldn't imagine caring so much about a hanger or a shelf.

"You're going running again?" Thomas spoke from under his pillow. That was his third time asking her that this week. Had she not ran before? It seemed, to her, the natural thing to do early in the morning.

"Yes" is what she simply said on previous days, but today, she added, "do you need something" and wished she hadn't said it just as quickly as it slipped from her lips.

"Finally" he shouted. Naked as the day he was born; Thomas jumped out of bed, walked over to the closet and grabbed his robe. When did he get undressed Diane thought? She remembered him wearing pajamas to bed, the ones with the ugly green golf clubs. Had they made love and she just couldn't remember? Maybe he got hot during the night she thought hopefully.

"I've been waiting for you to ask me that; I thought that I was going to have to teach you how to be my wife all over again." Thomas said with a chuckle. He smacked her on the butt as he headed towards the shower. Diane followed him wondering what he meant by "teaching her".

"Well, what is it that you want Thomas."

"Breakfast, my usual" he shouted over the pouring water. Diane just stood there thinking. She hasn't cooked anything since she'd been home; the corner café had become her friend. Thomas heard her silence and slammed the shower door back to look at her. His body was well toned, strong and how the water glistened on his skin, made him appear to be every woman's dream. Diane wondered if his body was something that she used to adore.

"See, that's my problem with you, I'm tired of reminding you of everything." Diane tried not to appear stunned but her heavy breathing couldn't hide her fear. "I want hash browns, two eggs over easy, two slices of lightly toasted rye bread and four link sausages." He closed the shower door. "I can't wait until this amnesia shit is over with." Diane didn't know if Thomas was aware that she'd heard him or not and somehow she didn't think he cared. Unfortunately, Diane was getting used to his comments about her condition; she just wished that his evilness was just as easy to swallow.

By the time Thomas had showered and dressed for work, Diane had fried the potatoes, toasted the bread, fried one two three four sausages and destroyed six eggs. She couldn't remember how to cook eggs over easy for the life of her. "I killed about a dozen hens trying to cook your eggs" she laughed as Thomas poured his coffee. "I just couldn't get it..."

"Enough" he interrupted. "How can you forget something you've done every day for the past six years?" He rose up to approach her, backing Diane into the refrigerator. How can I not remember a husband she wanted to say? Or why their relationship was obviously estranged. She didn't remember the feel of him, the scent of him or even a loving sound from his colossal voice. When he picked her up from the hospital, she was told that it was the first time he'd visited her in the three months that she was admitted. Yes he had called to secure the hospital bill but what kind of husband would stay in Miami, on a business trip after his wife had been beaten into a coma.

Thomas went on. "A good wife would have at least scrambled some eggs instead of leaving her husband with nothing." Thomas was practically nose to nose with Diane. She could smell the black coffee on his tongue. Diane didn't want to fear this man, husband or not, but most of all she didn't want to view herself as weak.

"A good husband would understand." She said sternly. The words had come out with so much conviction that even Diane believed them.

Thomas didn't blink; a smile began to curl the corners of his mouth and Diane began to think that finally they were going to see eye to eye on some things. She was just about to exhale when Thomas suddenly grabbed her face with one hand, squeezing her jaws so tightly, that she was certain he could feel the prints of her teeth in his hands.

"You are absolutely right. A good husband would." He let her go with a shove, bumping her head on the refrigerator and turned away laughing. "Your memory is worse than I thought." Thomas hated that their arrangement had been interrupted so abruptly; they had plans and her condition is a total disappointment. Diane stared at his breakfast on the table, rubbing her cheeks as she listened to Thomas's laugh fade into the garage.

"The Lord is my shepherd, the Lord is my shepherd" Diane whispered as she wondered 'how did I get here'.

The coffee shop was pretty noisy for a place that's supposed to be laid back. It was groups of people talking everywhere; at corner tables, on the sofa's and even standing in corners. Diane didn't want to complain for she left her house to get away from the quiet truth that was surrounding her, picking at the pores in her head, trying to get in and make her face them head on.

The walk over to the café was nice however; the warm August breeze was welcoming around the hems of her skirt and her toes appreciated the attention as well. As neighbors nodded their heads in greetings she wondered how many of them did she really know? Did they know her condition she thought? Did they stay away from her because of it or were they always distant?

After Thomas left, she carefully raided his home office. Everything was so neatly placed that Diane found herself dusting everything that she touched as if she was a criminal. In her search she discovered that Thomas was in financing and they were married in Rio six years ago. She couldn't find her birth certificate so her age is still a mystery to her. The deed to the house was signed and dated by her, a week before she was attacked. Were they living in a bad neighborhood? Had she walked in on a random burglary? Memories of that night still escape her and Thomas refuses to tell her anything, promising, "due to the trauma", that it's best that she doesn't remember. "But what about my memories before that" she'd ask. "Not much worth remembering before you met me" he'd laugh, leaving Diane to ponder over what he could be hiding.

For a while she'd thought he was right. Every photo in the house was of them. Even the photo albums were filled with pictures of them in Rio, London or someplace far from Savanna. Not one picture seemed to be of a friend or relative. Where was her family? Did she hate them all? Why didn't anyone come to assist her in her time of need? Do they all hate her?

"Oh my lord it is you!" A robust lady was standing in front of Diane teary eyed and beaming as if she'd found a lost child.

"Excuse me." Diane asked looking around the room. Some patrons were looking at the round woman, but most of them were busy drinking their "Grande mocha" this or "Venti caramel" that, with conversations circled around laptops and books, ranging from stocks and bonds to college craze parties coming up for the weekend.

"It's me, Nurse Barbra, from the hospital. I was at the counter over there..." she pointed to an empty seat at the counter. "...just looking and looking and I thought 'that could be her but her nose is different' and then you turned this way a little and bam, it was you." She excitedly hit the table making Diane jump. Nurse Barbra sat in the seat next to her and she seemed familiar but Diane wasn't fully aware of who she was. "Well I guess my feelings shouldn't be too hurt, you did go through a lot.

"You were my nurse?"

"Yeah child, for about two months." Barbra energy was amazing; she chuckled, pulled her jacket off and laid it and her purse on the seat across from Diane.

"I'm sorry I don't quite remember," Diane said politely.

"I'm sure you don't, but you might remember my voice one day. See I took care of you while you were in your coma and I talked to you all the time. I only got to see you once when you woke up and then those bastards changed my shift." She sucked through her teeth and shook her head. "Upper management is always messing up somebody's schedule. Hump, I'm lucky I got a job right." She giggled and sipped her latte.

Nurse Barbra started filling Diane in on information about her children and grandchildren as if they were old friends and to her surprise, Diane was beginning to remember some of the things she was saying. It gave her goose bumps just to hear her talk. "So did little Michael ever get his bike?" Diane chimed in happy to have remembered something. She was excited to have a conversation with someone other than Thomas. Nurse Barbra stopped talking, grabbed Diane's hand and patted it on the back.

"I knew it would work. I just knew it." She sniffled a bit.

"Barbra did anyone ever visit me?" Diane was afraid to ask but right now, Barbra was her only source of information. Barbra's face saddened a bit "No." She seemed to feel Diane's pain. "But your husband was there every night reading to you."

"My husband was there?" Diane couldn't believe it.

"Yes why are you surprised?"

"It's just that... well, the way he... he's never mentioned it that's all." Diane looked away to hide her confusion. Thomas told her that he arrived in from Miami the day that she was released.

"Well I don't see why not, that's something to be proud of. He came every night for about two hours and read the bible to you." She began to gather her things. "I think I even saw him praying. Those were the best two-hour breaks I ever had." She rose to leave.

"You're leaving?" Diane panicked. She wanted more information.

"Yes my dear, I have so much to do today." Barbra paused and noted the sadness that came across Diane's face. "Here" She took out a business card and gave it to Diane. "Call me anytime, I mean anytime." Diane nodded her head then stood to give the woman a hug.

"Thank you Barbra."

"Girl, don't make me cry." She turned to leave.

"Oh, Barbra" Diane shouted after her. Barbra stopped before reaching the door. "Did I seem to have nightmares when I was... sleeping?" Barbra looked confused for a moment then replied.

"You slept like a baby" she winked and left the coffee shop. Interesting woman Diane thought. She looked at the card she'd given her and it read; don't make beauty an issue, no hair style is too tough. Call Barbra before it gets too rough. Diane laughed to herself. She could hear the voice of the "diva-fied" nurse as clear as day.

Diane suddenly felt a chill run down her spine. Her ears were getting warm and she could even feel the hairs standing up on her neck. What was it? Panicking, Diane looked around the room searching for something familiar. Everyone there seemed as strange as her own reflection in the mirror that morning. Then she smelled a familiar scent. She couldn't pin point the source but it made her feel at peace or even safe as an old memory.

"Amen," a voice laughed from behind her. A man was at the counter smiling and laughing with the cashier. A familiar laugh to Diane but she didn't recognize his face. He saw her watching and seemed surprised to see her, he smiled. Diane's chests tighten when he began to head her way. Did he know her? Was he a relative, an old lover or maybe a friend of Thomas's? The pounding in her chest grew louder the closer he got to her.

"Well, you look great!" The man said stopping at her table. Diane tried not to get too excited too soon. She smiled lightly.

"Do I know you?" She asked but inside several other questions was raiding her thoughts; how did he know her and for how long, where did she come from and was Thomas her real husband but she didn't want to sound crazy. The man seemed to have paused to choose his words carefully.

"I believe I've seen you around before." He said gesturing towards the seat across from her. She nods her approval for him to sit.

"Like, where?" Diane watched the man as he settled into his seat. He wasn't too tall, brown skinned, medium build and his hair looked freshly trimmed. She could tell that he was fit because he was nervously rubbing his tie down against his stomach, which Diane noticed, didn't have any roundness or plumpness to it.

"You're... um, Thomas Crawford's wife aren't you?" He watched her eyes as she answered; she looked sad and confused and he realized that maybe her memory hadn't returned.

"Yes, Diane. She reached to shake his hand. He seemed reluctant for a moment but he gently shook her hand, he almost held it Diane thought. It was soft in a way and warm. The heat gave her goose bumps so she quickly pulled away. Why did she feel this way about this stranger? Diane got the feeling as if they were forbidden lovers who finally got a chance to be alone. The hairs on the back of her neck were still standing, her arms were prickling and her heart hadn't stopped racing since he walked over to her table.

"Are you a friend of Thomas's?" Diane looked around the room trying to get her thoughts off of her nerves. She turned her attention back to the man who hadn't answered yet, and who appeared to be offended by her question.

"No, I'm not a friend. I've never met the man." He smiled from the corner of his mouth trying to lighten the mood. "I've seen your picture in the paper or magazine somewhere." Diane was about to ask which paper but he seemed to purposely cut her off.

"Where are my manners? I'm Terrance Crosby" He reached to shake her hand again but Diane didn't move.

"So did you see me around somewhere or did you see me in the paper?" A different since of nervousness came over her. What an idiot she thought. I'm a victim of a violent attack with amnesia as a result, a stranger gives me goose bumps and all I think is that he may have been my lover, Diane screamed in her head. "I'm sorry but I have to go." She starts to gather her things. Crosby stands to help her, mentally kicking himself for not taking a more cautious approach. The woman has been through a lot already and fearing him was the last thing he wanted. He wanted to assure her that she was safe with at least him, if no one else.

"Nice meeting you Mrs. Crawford," he reached to shake her hand once more and to his surprise, she responded. Maybe she did it to be polite, or to prove to herself that she wasn't scared, but she shook his hand and looked into his eyes. "I would never hurt you" Crosby said quietly.

Diane slowly pulled her hand away but something about his voice made her believe him. "Have a good day." She smiled, turned and left the coffee shop. Crosby watched her through the window mentally darting down his mistakes. He couldn't afford to have her afraid of him. He needed her memory back just as much as she did and he needed her to be comfortable with him, someone that she could confide in. He'd worked too hard these last few months to lose her trust by moving too fast.

He'd almost put all the pieces together, to the point of knowing that it was one out of two men, or both from a parcel shoe print of blood he found in the bathroom and finger prints on a drinking glass that hasn't shown up in the system but definitely belonging to a man. Thomas Crawford's finger prints were everywhere, but the fact that he lived there they meant nothing, however in the same, it doesn't exempt him of charges either.

LOST AND FOUND   CHAPTER THREE

Thomas took the last bite of his toasted rye bread covered in egg yolk from his perfectly fried eggs over easy. Although the food was good, coming to this restaurant for three weeks has been a bit of an inconvenient. Not only did he have to get up earlier in the mornings, he also had to pay his driver overtime. He hated his driver's smug ego but now it's gotten worse with the extra money he's been paying him.

The diner was basic; squared tables set for four, with checkered board table cloths that's been cleaned so many times that the patterns were beginning to fade. Pictures of various locations in New York hung on the wall which Thomas didn't doubt needed a fresh coat of paint. He could smell the grease in the walls and the floor had a black and white checkered pattern that turned into spirals if you stared too long.

There were regular customers at the counter, gentlemen that Thomas, in his own inside joke, referred to them as the retirement crew. Each one would come in one after the other with a newspaper tucked under his arm. They'd all order coffee first as they read the paper, then they'd order food. Probably something they were trained to do while waiting for their wives to cook breakfast, Thomas chuckled.

Although the menu hasn't changed in the three weeks that he's been there, the retirement crew would take about ten minutes to order. Tammy, the lone waitress, would just pour their coffee, and then ignore them for about fifteen minutes. Thomas even noticed that when she took their orders, she never wrote anything down. Thomas guessed that they'd been coming in longer than they, themselves, could remember. All the other regulars seemed as normal as he hoped he was. A couple of cops sat in the corner booth, a dancer, he learned by eavesdropping, sat near the door and a nurse, getting off nightshift, would come in every other day and smile at him a little too much, he thought.

He looked out at his driver, Greg Young, who was now standing outside the car. Thomas knew that he was getting antsy because it was close to the time he took his wife or girlfriend or something, to work. He didn't care though because the way Thomas figured it, he paid Greg enough for him to buy his wife a car. Better yet, he paid him enough to let her stay home. What people did with their money was beyond anything that Thomas could comprehend.

"Would that be all Sir?" the waitress's squeaky shoes warned him that she was coming. He didn't answer, as usual. Thomas took out a twenty dollar bill and placed it in her grease stained apron. Although his tab was only ten dollars, she never asked if he wanted his change. Tammy cleared his table, mumbled a thank you, and then went to tend to a gentleman at the end of the counter. "I'll be with you in a moment detective." She smiled and bumped him with her hip. The man laughed then looked up at Thomas. Thomas didn't recognize the detective so he just nodded his head "hello", and left Tammy another tip, a habit he started when he overheard her tell someone that her car broke down. He didn't want to have to break in a new waitress, explaining what he wanted or even how he wanted it. He also didn't like how servers always ask "Is everything ok over here?" so he would definitely have to set that straight before even ordering.

The detective seemed to watch him as he was leaving Thomas thought which concerned him. After Diane's incident he made sure that all his clients were still in the game and reassured all the nervous ones that Diane hadn't talked. He had Greg sneak a peek at him to see if he'd seen him around but claimed that he's never seen him before but he made it a rule to only believe every other thing that any man had to say.

"Has anybody been in here asking questions about me?" Thomas asked firmly, startling the elderly lady sitting at the receptionist desk. Mary was used to his yelling and his childish stomping from time to time but this time he seemed frightened and a frightened man can easily become a desperate man, Mary thought.

"No sir", she said touching the gold frame that housed a photo of her grandchildren, it calmed her on days such as this. Looking at their lovely smiles, on their vacation to Hawaii, reminds her of why she has tolerated Thomas all these years. She jumped up to hang his coat and hat, that he barely gave her time to grab hold of as he tossed it in her direction. She followed him to his office "just your usual clients and here are your banquet tickets for tonight". Some clients she thought. They all appeared to be goons to her; ill-mannered and they always smelled like cigar ashes. Thomas stopped in his tracks and turned to look Mary in her eyes.

"Are you sure?" she nodded her head. "How about any new clients?" Mary thought a moment then shook her head. Thomas paused a moment longer, then relaxed his shoulders. "Take a letter in ten minutes and not a minute less. And please remind my wife about tonight's benefit, I want her ready when I get there." Thomas shut his office door leaving Mary to smell the wood in front of her face.

"Ten, nine, eight... two, one." Mary counted before she moved. That boy has the manners of a jackass she wanted to say out loud. It was hard for her to believe he had a mother. Mary returned to her desk and smiled at the secret her and detective Crosby was keeping. Crosby had come by the office two evenings ago but Mary, knowing something was strange about Thomas Crawford's business associates, agreed not to mention the detective's visit or his questions: "how long he been in business? How many clients he had? How much he grossed a week? Did he visit his wife in the hospital?" Whatever Mr. Crawford was doing in the dark was sure to come to light. And if providing fresh batteries to detective Crosby's flashlight was helpful, then why not, she was ready to retire anyway.

Crosby took the last bite of his breakfast, sipped his coffee and paid Tammy. She would always look at him after counting out his bills as if it should be more. How much of a tip should one get for passing off grits and toast from the kitchen window to the counter, he thought. Maybe she needed extra money for some reason he thought. He made a mental note to leave a bigger tip next time.

The elderly gentlemen at the end of the counter were quietly arguing as usual. The shorter one who's oversized mole sitting on his right temple, was rising and falling as he raced to finish chewing his pancakes, so that he might add to the bogus political statement his comrade just stated; he always had to have the last word. The one in the middle, Mr. Edwards, who appeared to be older than the others, would pretend to read the paper during these arguments while throwing in instigative words or comments as his friends went at it. The third guy would argue vigorously with the shorter guy until he was all red and bothered. But then he'd always end it with, "you're probably right". "Of course I'm right" the shorter guy would conclude. They called him chubby, a name he must have gained for himself back in the day because the coffee mug he was holding seemed to outweigh him.

"Good morning detective" a sultry voice on long legs stood so close to him that he could breathe in every dab of her 360 degrees, so he knew exactly who those legs belonged to. That Perry Elis perfume was dabbed twice behind the ear, once in the crescent of her bosom, because odors floated upwards, and a dab each, on the sides of her bikini line. Just as he used to watch Pamela dress, and watched those long legs wrap around him every night for two years, his heart still pounded as he watched those same legs slowly cross on the bar stool next to him.

"What do you want?" Crosby mumbled.

"Oh wow! I don't get a good morning in return? I'm sure you miss me more than that." Pamela swung her legs in his direction; for sure torture, Crosby was convinced. Legs he's seen a million times on his sofa, across his bed and wrapped around his waist when she was happy. Crosby tried to focus on her face but even that was still beautiful enough to make him stutter. Her skin was smooth, a flawless milk chocolate complexion that Richard Barthe himself couldn't improve upon. Her teeth were white but not too bright where the realism faded. Pamela's long lashes and eyebrows were nicely manicured as sure were her toe nails and the hair around her 'awesome spot' she called a place that he used to call home. Her short, naturally curly afro was shiny and inviting, her best feature he thought, that even now, Crosby wanted to touch it.

"What do you want Pamela, I'm sure that you didn't come here for the food?" he looked away and started counting the patrons in the restaurant, a habit he started in order to fight the power of being pulled in by a beautiful woman. It was twenty people in the coffee shop the day he saw Diane Crawford. Twenty-one if you count the man standing outside the door who appeared to be waiting on someone.

"Is that any way to treat your fiancé?"

"Ex-fiancé, you weren't good at that remember." Pamela smiled at the thought of her "so called" business trips to Miami. As far as she was concerned, Terrance had no physical evidence of her cheating. He only assumed which part of her trip was business and which part was pleasure. She had her story and she was sticking to it.

"Still bitter I see. Did you ever solve that case that broke us apart?" Crosby didn't answer. "Oh, I forgot. Discussing a case is not an option." She mocked.

Crosby flinched. Deep down, he knew that keeping Pamela out of his work relations may have been a big part of her unfaithfulness. Not sharing everything with the woman in your life could lead her into feeling un-needed. That was a lesson from his granny that he'd forgotten. The very reason he needed to come clean with Diane; he wanted her to trust him to no end.

"Look, if you want something say it, otherwise I have some place to be." Pamela smile faded as Crosby stood up to leave.

"No it's cool" she stood in front of him and cupped her breast to push them upward. Something she knew Crosby couldn't resist. Nine, ten... twelve patrons he counted. "I have a trip to pack for anyway" Pamela grabbed her purse off the counter and paused. "I just thought that you might want to see me is all. Pamela leaned in to give Crosby a kiss but he pulled away from her. "I guess not" she laughed and headed towards the door. A black car pulled up but she didn't allow the driver to get out. Just before her long legs disappeared into the car Crosby called from the cafe doorway.

"Miami?"

Pamela winked her eye at him and closed the door. The driver sped off immediately. K40 2598, a license Crosby knew he'll never forget.

The banquet hall was the most elegant place Diane had ever seen; the golden pillars looked as if they were brought directly from Rome, the marble floor was glistening from the many candles that decorated the walls enhancing the ancient art that hung there and the centerpieces on each table were of beautiful vases that stood at least twenty-five inches from the table filled with beautiful bouquets of flowers. And the ball gown that she found in her closet was gold and graced with pearls and rhinestones, or maybe even real diamonds, made her feel like the party was in her honor.

"Damn, close your mouth and act like you've been here before." Thomas was smiling as people walked passed greeting them but Diane could taste the venom in his words. "These people have to believe that your memory is fine and the Diane Crawford that they knew, hated these functions because it made her feel nervous and on the spot so act accordingly." Thomas kissed her lovingly on the cheek and excused himself to go speak to an elderly gentleman whom everyone seemed to cater to. The gentleman saw Thomas approach and dismissed everyone with the wave of his hand. Thomas spoke close to the man's ear; they laughed and then headed over towards Diane.

"Diane, it is so lovely to see you and you're looking more gorgeous than all the women in here as usual." He laughed at himself but Thomas laughed harder giving Diane the impression that this man was important to Thomas.

"Judge McAfee, I wouldn't let Mrs. McAfee hear that if I were you." Thomas gestured towards a plump lady in a black dress who seemed to be getting catered to as well.

"Well you're not me and a woman like Diane needs to be praised and celebrated. I have no idea why you don't throw her one of these galas yourself" Judge McAfee slightly frowned at Thomas as he grabbed Diane's arm to dance. Diane sensed Thomas's embarrassment and tried to lighten the mood.

"Oh Judge, you know how I hate these functions, they always make me feel nervous and on the spot."

"Then I guess Thomas has to find some other way to please you. Shall we dance? I've been waiting on you all night." Judge McAfee and Diane laughed leaving Thomas standing in a pool of guilt that he could only smirk at and Diane hoped he wouldn't take it out on her later. "I hope everything is still going according to plan." The Judge stated when they were safely in the center of the ballroom floor.

"Why wouldn't it be" was all Diane could think to say. It was obvious that the three of them had some kind of business together and Diane's input was more important than Thomas's to the Judge or maybe it was a secret of theirs alone.

"Good, glad to hear. I'm sorry about your incident by the way; if I could have prevented it from happening, I would have."

"It's nice to know that someone cares about me." Diane wondered how he could have prevented a robbery. Well, as far as she knew, it was a robbery but she was told that nothing was missing. Whatever they were looking for wasn't something she could have just handed to them or she's sure that she would have.

"Is Thomas mistreating you...?"

"No, no it's not that at all." Diane interrupted. She wouldn't dare tell anyone that her husband was mistreating her. Even with her having amnesia, she knew better than that. Her granny always taught the women in her family to never embarrass your man. Diane gasped at that thought. How does she remember what her granny said but not her granny, not even the image of her face or the tone of her voice? Diane began to wonder if she had a granny at all or was she just imagining it, creating a family of hope.

"So were you?" the Judge was saying pulling Diane from her thoughts.

"I'm sorry, what was that?"

"Were you able to make that last transaction before your incident?" Judge McAfee was now glaring at her sternly. Did he know that she had no idea of what he was referring to? What kind of transaction would a judge concern himself with let alone a transaction with her? Was she a partner with with Thomas in the finance business? Should she just tell him that...?

"There he goes again, always talking business at the wrong time" a sultry voice interrupted them on the dance floor. She was beautiful Diane thought, almost flawless if it wasn't for the eerie feeling that she was receiving from this woman with a split in her dress almost to her navel. "Diane, do you mind if I steal him for a moment?" The woman smiled knowingly at the women around the room who looked at her before allowing their glance to move quickly and accusingly at their escorts, who themselves could neither ignore this woman, nor look away fast enough to avoid a certain problem when they got home that evening. She made the women in the room wish they had played harder or smarter or else stayed home.

"No, of course I don't mind." The Judge smiled at Diane as he took the other woman into his arms to dance. Diane quickly excused herself and searched for a restroom. All the faces in the room seem to be swarming towards her. Everyone was calling her name and smiling and the room was spinning in her mind so much that she felt dizzy and lost her footing, bumping into detective Crosby. "I'm so sorry..." Diane stopped short, recognizing the man in front of her. "Umm...?"

"Terrance Crosby, we met at the coffee house today." Crosby held his hand out to shake Diane's but when she noticed Thomas approaching, she didn't reciprocate. Diane was relieved to see the women's lounge area and rushed away without saying a word but Thomas cut her off at the door and led her to the front entrance.

"Let's go before something goes wrong." Thomas seemed nervous but Diane couldn't focus on that. What was Terrance Crosby doing there she thought. Was he following her or was her first thought of him correct, that he was her lover. Most people, who cheat, keep their lovers in the same circle and with a crowd such as this, she was sure that she wasn't the only one cheating.

Before he realized it, Crosby had followed Diane and Thomas out to the lobby. He hoped that he hadn't caused her any added injury to the obvious ailing relationship she had with her husband if they were truly married at all.

"You sure do know how to make a woman run" Pamela whispered behind Crosby's ear.

"I thought that you were going to Miami."

"No, you said that I was going to Miami. I said that I had to pack for a trip and if I recall correctly, I never said when I was leaving." Crosby turned to look at the voice he knew all too well and wished that he hadn't. The split in Pamela's dress made him remember even the taste of her, let alone how she felt in his arms and there was no way that he'd be able to count the people in this room before losing his cool. Crosby was always amazed by her beauty that kept him speechless in another life and still, in this life, her control turned him on even more. With all that he could muster, he tipped his hat in her honor and walked away.

LOST AND FOUND   CHAPTER SIX

Thomas dried his legs and arms as he watched Diane sleeping. She was beautiful with her creamy brown skin, a freckle here and there, long brown hair and a deep dimple on the left side of her mouth that drew you in instantly. What a waste he thought; she used to be so freaky, but yet, so easy to tame. Thomas rubbed the erection that was now growing between his legs and decided to give Diane another chance to do what a wife is supposed to do.

Thomas gently pulled back the covers to expose the laced boy shorts he ordered her to sleep in last night; he didn't want her then, he was just testing her obedience. He slide in behind her and cupped her breast while he slowly grinded his erection against the lace. He moved her hair back exposing her ear and began to lick it with the tip of his tongue. Diane moaned when he began to gingerly run his hand down the front of her thigh. He was being so gentle, so succulent and the hardness that pressed against her butt made her voluntarily open her legs. Maybe he's starting to love me again she thought. Maybe, just maybe after this, he'll help me remember something. Diane turned over on top of him, grabbing hold of his eagerness while rubbing him softly.

"That's it baby. You know what I like" he moaned. Diane lowered herself to feel his warm tongue on her breast, she shivered. His fingertips were cool on her back as he pulled her in for more but it made everything else warm and wet. Thomas slid her down his body so that he could feel her moisture. She moaned and shivered just as she used to. It turned him on more to know that he could do that to her. He began to wildly kiss her neck as she rolled and twisted her hips looking for an orgasm.

He forcefully grabbed her and brought her to a kiss. He began to lick her lips and thrust his tongue inside her mouth. His mouth tasted of metal Diane thought, so she turned away and began to kiss his neck, it was sour. Thomas slid her panties to the side and thrust himself inside her. Diane bucked and gasped, Thomas felt like cold unbending steel. She sat up hoping the adjustment would soften but he turned them both over and began pounding away.

Diane closed her eyes and tried to focus on something pleasant. She recited "The lord is my shepherd", over and over in her head until a vision of her sitting at a table, in the middle of a field of rocks came to mind. The closer she walked towards the sun light her thoughts of Thomas had dissipated. As she was about to step into the light no one pulled her hair this time. She turned to look at the darkness behind her and a giant hand slammed across her face.

"Ouch!" Diane sat up screaming and holding her face. Thomas was kneeled over her and wiping himself with a towel.

"I should slap you again. Do you know how hard it is to release while you're saying a prayer and drying up on me?" He tossed the towel on her stomach and headed to the bathroom. Diane was confused, had she blacked out? Was Thomas the person in her dream pulling her back from the light? What doesn't he want her to know? Why does she block out their intimate moments?

"I don't understand you" she shouted.

"You don't understand me?" Thomas stormed back into the room and stopped at the foot of the bed. "And furthermore, who in the hell are you yelling at." Diane shook her head. Thomas bumped the bed with his knee to scare her.

"I'm sorry Thomas." She pleaded. "It's just that a nurse from the hospital said you came to read to me every night so naturally..."

"A nurse said what?" Thomas stopped buttoning his shirt.

"She said that no one visited me but my husband." Thomas looked at Diane and thought for a minute. Suddenly his eyes widened and his breathing got heavy. Diane threw the towel to the floor and grabbed her t-shirt and shorts from the foot of the bed. Thomas paced back and forward in front of the bed as Diane carefully dressed. She knew that she'd never make it to the door but she'd be more confident fighting back with some clothes on.

"You bitch!" Thomas said through clenched teeth and lunged toward Diane. She jumped on the bed and ran across to the other side. Thomas fell on top of the bed and quickly jumped up to come around to the other side. Diane was trapped between Thomas's anger, the bed and the window.

"What are you talking about?" she screamed. Thomas reached for her as she tried to run across the bed again. Diane began kicking him with her left leg as he pulled her to the floor with her right. She reached out and punched him. He didn't flinch and the look he gave her, dared her to do it again. Diane's head bounced on the carpet as Thomas' knees pinned her arms to the floor.

"You've been cheating on me, again" It was more of a statement then a question. Shocked, Diane answered no. "You're lying. Who came to visit you?" he demanded.

"You did Thomas, you!" Diane cried. Thomas jumped up and pulled Diane onto the bed.

"You're a liar." Thomas pulled off his belt, flipped Diane over, placed his knee on her back and began to whip her. "Who came to see you?"

"I don't know" she screamed trying to get away. Thomas angrily whipped her several more times before coming to a stop. Diane's screams had long faded, her fears flew away with every swing of his belt and anger was now living inside her. If Thomas would beat her twenty more times, Diane doubt she would even feel it.

Thomas sat on the edge of the bed trying to catch his breath. "Who came to visit you Diane?" she wiped the saliva from her mouth and sat up in pain.

"I was in a coma asshole." Diane didn't know what was going to happen next, but nothing else seemed befitting. Thomas looked at her and chuckled.

"Oh yeah, you were." He said. Diane watched him get dressed as if nothing happened. Is this her fault she thought? Had he done this to her six years ago and she let him get away with it? Diane gasped at her next thought, was Thomas himself her attacker. Thomas turned to her "I don't know how much longer I can tolerate you."

"Tolerate!" Diane's attitude couldn't be suppressed. Thomas shook his finger at her, to watch her tone, as if she was a child.

"Yes tolerate; put up with... deal with... be bothered with." He sucked his teeth and finished tying his tie and then he went to the closet to retrieve a suitcase. "Why won't you just live in the moment? What is this persistent need to remember the past? Stop asking me about friends, parents and dogs and shit."

Diane tried to hold back her tears to no avail; she didn't care how many tears fell, as long as she didn't start those stupid, little 'hick-upping' spasms. It made her feel so weak. "Why do you hate me?" Diane whined despite her will. She wanted to sound strong and assuring but her emotions of feeling unwanted wouldn't let her.

"I don't hate you. Hell, I made you into the woman that you are." Thomas began to pack underwear and t-shirts into his suitcase. Diane didn't care where he was going, how long he'd be gone was more important.

"In fact, when I found you, you were nothing and no one, not even your family wanted you." Thomas mentally kicked himself for mentioning her family. He knew she'd never shut up about it now but Diane didn't say a word because she could see by Thomas's body language that he didn't mean to expose that bit of information. She had a family out there somewhere and for some reason, Thomas wants her to think that she is all alone. Diane quietly watched Thomas pack the last of his things and hoped he'll be leaving soon. She decided to go into the kitchen to make herself busy so Thomas wouldn't see how eager she was for him to leave, for her determination to find information just got stronger

Diane went into the kitchen to make a pot of coffee, when she reached for the coffee pot it turned into a Wine rack. Diane jumped back closed her eyes shaking her head to the confusion. When she opened her eyes the coffee pot had reappeared. Diane grabbed hold of the counter top to keep from falling to the floor. Was she losing her mind or was this a flash back she thought in fear. She shook off her fear and thought about her mission.

Diane could hear her husband wheeling his suitcase towards the kitchen. She stood at the porch doors and casually glared out the window. Her heart was racing as she mentally went through each box in Thomas's office. She prayed something was there to guide her home. "I'll be back on Saturday" he said heading towards the garage. "And you know what else." Thomas stopped to look at his wife standing in the window. Diane didn't dare look at him. She wanted his image to be gone for good. "You wasn't shit when I found you and you won't be nothing without me. So you should be glad for your 'so called' amnesia."

Diane felt her neck heating up. She may have once enjoyed a lavish apartment or this huge house, but if 'nothing' was something she had to become in order to rid of Thomas, then hell or high waters wasn't going to stop her. She had five days to find herself, being here on day six was not an option.

Diane stood in the window until she heard Thomas place his suitcase in the trunk and close it; the driver door open and close; the ignition start –which was soft so it meant he was taking her car instead of his truck; and the garage door open and close. She even waited until she could no longer hear the tires turning on the pavement before she moved away from the window.

Diane put her mug down on the kitchen table and headed straight to Thomas's office. She pushed the door open and looked around. Everything was in neat piles or stacks on his desk and on the book cases. If she'd touch anything he was sure to know but who cared, she'd be long gone before he gets back.

Diane started pulling out drawers, looking between the books lined on the shelf, in the file cabinet and behind it. She found nothing. Maybe his office was just too obvious she thought. Barefooted she walked through the kitchen to the garage. After the automated lights were completely on, Diane rushed to a huge tool box on the shelf.

The box was too heavy to move so she grabbed a ladder from the wall, opened it and climbed two steps to be leveled with the tool box and found that it had a combination lock on it. As she looked around for something to break the lock, Diane broke out into hysterical laughter. "I know the combination" she smiled. It was her birthday. She didn't know how she remembered that but she did." Left-three, right-twenty two, left..." she paused. Eighty eight was the last number but the lock only went up to forty five. "Think Diane. Think." She mentally crossed her fingers and dialed left-eight, the lock popped.

Diane almost fell over backward when she opened the box; several bonds filled the tool box and she began to shake. What kind of life was Thomas leading? Or even her-self? As she flipped through the bonds she found the name of a woman she didn't know typed on most of them and her name on the others. She slammed the box shut and locked it. Why did Thomas have these bonds in someone else name and why would he give her the combination.

She quickly continued her search. Diane pulled down several boxes from the shelves. She found deeds to properties in Savannah, Chicago and New York. A ledger of houses bought and sold, and pictures of Thomas with men in suits she didn't recognize and photos of Thomas and Judge McAfee were also in the boxes. She even found a lease to an apartment in Miami.

When Diane pulled herself up from the pile of papers she felt numb, she found nothing to link her to her past. Not a birth certificate, birthday card or even a piece of mail from a previous address was found in the rubbish that now lay at her feet. She aimlessly wandered into the bathroom where she stared at the woman in the mirror.

"Who are you?" she questioned and waited a moment for an answer. Frustrated she took off her shorts and t-shirt and stood in front of the full length mirror. "Who do I look like?" she asked "Is this my daddy's nose or my mom's?" "Whose butt do I have?" she screamed.

Diane turned to look at her back in the mirror. She had purple and black bruises everywhere. She even had a whelp shaped like the tip of a belt on the side of her waste. Diane grabbed a hand mirror off the sink and angled it so that she could see her whole back. She began to tremble at the sight. Diane could see dark marks, in rows, across her back. She'd been beaten before and it wasn't with a belt.

She turned to the full length mirror again and demanded "Who the hell are you?" She pressed her face against it to look into the eyes of the woman that stared back. "Are those your eyes?" she stepped back and spat at the mirror. "Bitch, you're a liar." She started pulling out her eyebrows. "I can't tolerate you. I'm tired of your shit, Diane. Is that even your name?" The hand mirror dropped to the floor, shards of glass nestled into the crevices of the ceramic floor tile as Diane began pulling out her hair. "Speak up. Who are you? Who are you?" she started slapping herself as strands of hair fell to the floor.

"Ok, you won't talk. I got something for you." She headed towards the front door. She fumbled with the locks as tears filled her eyes and desperation set in. Diane ran out into the middle of the street and screamed. "Who am I?" she ran to the house across the street and banged on the door. She crossed the yard and rang the bell next door. An old man stepped out of the first house shocked at the nude woman running towards him.

"Wait, do you know me" Diane pleaded. He shook his head no and Diane began to scream louder and louder. Neighbors were beginning to emerge shaking their heads and covering their mouths in shock. Diane stopped screaming and collapsed in her neighbors' yard. As she laid there in a fetal position, trying to catch her breath, she could hear the murmuring from the people asking where did she come from.

"Someone please get the child a blanket" an elderly lady said. As a hush grew over the crowd, someone put a coat over her and Diane smiled within. Someone did care about her. The coat had a familiar scent of sandal wood. Something she smelled not too long ago. Immediately she sat up knowing exactly who the scent belonged to.

"Stay away from me" Diane shouted. An alarm of gasp went through the crowd. Crosby didn't want to tell her who he was, like this but under the circumstances, he had no choice.

"I'm detective Terrance Crosby, please stand back and give her some air." He held his badge in the air so everyone could see it. He didn't want to risk a mob attack.

Someone yelled, "Detective, you better be. You need to see that she gets a doctor."

"I'll take care of her" Crosby tried to pull Diane to her feet. She resisted more, so he let her hand go and sat in the grass behind her with one leg on each side of her, cuddling her. He slowly placed his arms around her and rocked her back and forward as you would do a baby.

Diane tried to break away but he wouldn't let her. "Do you know what you're doing detective?" someone asked. Crosby ignored them then started to recite the twenty-third Psalms.

"The lord is my shepherd; I shall not want..." the more Crosby spoke, the calmer Diane got. "Surely goodness and mercy shall follow me all the days of my life: and I will dwell in the house of the lord forever."

"Detective, please take me home." Diane said softly. Crosby rose and helped Diane to her feet. There was a light applause as they walked to the Crawford's house. Diane stopped and turned to see her neighbors return to their homes as if nothing happened. She looked up at Crosby with a troubled smiled. "He said he found me."

Crosby smiled at the corner of his lips. "Let's just get you inside, and then we'll figure out how to get you out of the lost and found if you don't mind." Diane shook her head no and let him lead her inside the house.

Diane woke to the sound of a running shower and a man singing. She slowly sat up in the bed and went into an immediate panic. She was in a familiar hotel room but the man's voice was one that she didn't recognize. "Thomas" she called out uncertain of what was to come next. A voice that wasn't Thomas's called back "You say something Diane?" Diane shook her head and squeezed her eyes shut. She rubbed her eyes and then opened them slowly. She was still in the hotel room. She slowly looked around the room and as she turned to look in the other direction, the room slowly transformed back to her bedroom.

After catching her breath, she stood and looked in the mirror, almost wishing that she saw someone else. Her hair was pulled back into a ponytail, she had on a pair of pajama bottoms and a sweatshirt and she had a large bandage on the bottom of her right foot; none of which she remember doing herself. Diane remembered that the detective, Terrance Crosby, helped her into the house that morning but that was about it.

She carefully pulled on a pair of slippers and limped slightly through the house. The bathroom was clean, Thomas's office was neat again and things in the garage looked untouched; she exhaled with relief that the lock on the tool box was still secure. Diane dialed the combination, still amused that she remembered the numbers, and looked around for another hiding place for the bonds. Her eyes landed on the lawn mower. Diane quickly dumped the contents of the lawn mower bag out into the garbage can in the corner of the garage and just as quickly filled it with the bonds. She crumpled a few of them just in case someone was smart enough to feel the bag in their search and then added in some grass. Diane wondered what the detective found as he put her things back into place. She guessed that he had an obligation to the State of Georgia to do his job, didn't he? What placed him into her life? Was he investigating her or her husband?

Diane rushed back into her bedroom, grabbed her purse off the door knob and dumped the contents onto the bed. It looked like a typical female purse; red lipstick, eye shadows of Smokey grays and blues; a nail file, check book and address book. The check book told her that she had a balance of fifty-three thousand dollars on the day she was attacked. The address book was empty. In fact, it appeared to be brand new.

There wasn't a cell phone or a wallet in the pile which was odd. Was she robbed during the attack? What else was taken? She spotted the card nurse Barbra gave her and looked it over. It only had her personal business information on it and Diane desperately needed the name of the hospital. She reached further into the purse and pulled out a pink slip of paper. As she unfolded the paper, she let out a sigh of relief when above the word "discharge" she found the hospital's letterhead.

Diane repacked her purse and looked at the watch on her night stand. "Good, I have time to catch her before her shift starts." As she placed the watch on her wrist she experienced a déjà vu moment. She closed her eyes and tried to remember what was going to happen.

She's sitting on her bed somewhere getting dressed. Just as she's placing the watch on her wrist, someone snatches it off breaking the strap. It falls to the floor just as a man steps into the doorway...

She couldn't remember any more details so Diane grabbed her purse, a picture of Thomas from the office and then headed out to the garage. Her heart was racing as she drove to Memorial University Medical Center where she was hoping to find someone who recognized Thomas.

Thomas acted as though he hadn't visited her at all but Nurse Barbra said he had. Diane turned on her GPS system for she'd heard of Waters Avenue but she had no time to get lost. After asking a million questions, Diane finally reached the correct department. She had ten minutes left before nurse Barbra started her shift so she decided to find the department in which she was housed for months in her coma.

"Ma'am, we just can't let you inside of someone else's hospital room." The nurse explained for the second time.

"Please nurse... Jackie" Diane read her name tag. The nurse shook her head then started filling in a chart on the wall behind her desk. "I know you have your rules but, I was in a coma here for several months and I just wanted to see the room, try to get a feel of it, to see if I could remember something, anything." Diane took a deep breath and prayed the nurse would have some sympathy.

"Now if you wake Mrs. Burton I'm going to make you take care of her personally." Nurse Jackie coached as she guided Diane to the room. "That woman's a pistol and when she's sleeping, we're in heaven."

"Thank you so much" Diane said quietly. Nurse Jackie pushed the door open softly and ushered Diane in.

"Five minutes" she told her and headed back to the nurses' station. Diane quietly walked to the side of the bed and sat in the chair. She closed her eyes and tried to concentrate. There was nothing familiar about the sounds or smells but it was comfortable. Almost like a sanctuary.

"I come here to get away from my husband too." Mrs. Burton's cracking voice startled Diane.

"I'm so sorry. Did I wake you" she rose and stood beside the woman's bed.

"No dear. I just pretend to sleep to keep those busy nurses away." She laughed. Diane smiled. "Don't worry dear, everything will be just fine." She squeezed Diane's hand just as nurse Jackie peaked in to flag Diane out. Diane looked back at Mrs. Burton who appeared to be asleep and whispered a "thank you". Mrs. Burton smiled with her eyes still closed.

Diane sat in the waiting room of the labor and delivery department, watching eager dads and nervous grandparents pace the halls, awaiting a bouncing boy or a sparkling girl to add to their family photo albums.

Nurse Barbra had arrived an hour ago but was quickly called into the delivery room to hold a frighten teenagers hand. "Her parents make her more nervous." Barbra said before disappearing into the busy room. Nurse Barbra seemed to be an all-around friend Diane thought.

Diane closed her eyes to the sounds of new born babies, probably the sound of every mothers dream, in the beginning anyway. Without opening her eyes she could hear the happy family bustling to the recovery room, gasps of excitement and soft tears of a welcoming blessing.

"You know you really need to let me do those eyebrows of yours," Barbra said plopping down in the seat next to Diane.

"Yeah, well, I'm going to need some patch work done too." Diane laughed as she patted her head.

"Girl, what happened to you?"

"I had a fight with myself."

"Enough said" Barbra laughed. I fight with myself all the time. But I win. They both laughed like old friends would do. "Ok, what can I do for you? I know you're not sitting here, in the hospital, at midnight just for kicks." Diane took a deep breath and dug into her purse. She carefully laid the photo of Thomas on Barbra lap. Barbra lifted the picture, scanned the back of it then handed the photo back to Diane.

"So is that your brother or something? I think I seen him at the diner on west Henry Street before but..."

"No, he's my husband" Diane interrupted. Barbra frowned and took the photo from Diane. She looked at it frontwards, backwards an even upside down.

"I'm trying really hard Mrs. Crawford, but no matter how I angle it, this man, don't look anything like your husband." Barbra was about to laugh but Diane jumped up and began rushing down the corridor.

"Diane, wait! What's going on?" Barbra shouted. Diane didn't stop running until she reached the emergency room where she collapsed in the middle of the floor; out of breath and with added fear that she's been living with a stranger and whoever visited her in the hospital, could have very well been her attacker. The room was spinning and she effortlessly reached out to grab hold to something. The awaiting patients appeared busy but she could see by their expressions that she must look like an escaped mental patient.

"Security!" someone called out.

"No, I got her." Crosby grabbed Diane by her hands and pulled her up. "Diane, look at me" he demanded. She looked at detective Crosby and stared; her eyes were sad but her hands were steady. Crosby guided her to a chair next to the triage station. "Wait here for me." Diane began to pull away. Crosby softly placed his hand on her cheek and turned her to face him. "Please, I don't want to lose you." Diane nodded yes as tears streamed from her eyes.

"Ok, thank you. I need to finish some business with an injured offender and then I'll get you out of here." He handed her a folded sheet of paper. "I found this in Thomas's office." He turned to leave.

"Detective" Diane called to him.

"How many times will you come to my rescue?" She smiled.

"As many times as it take, amen" he chuckled.

"Amen" she agreed. Crosby stopped by the triage station then disappeared into a small room. The word "amen" continued to play over and over in Diane's head. "... in Jesus name amen." "God bless her and her family, where ever they may be. Amen." These phrases were playing fresh in her mind as if someone, Crosby, had just said them. "Please bless this beautiful creature from her coma lord. Amen." Diane gasped. It couldn't have been him she thought but that would explain why she knows his voice, his scent and the twenty-third Psalms; the verses he used to keep her calm, the verses she herself used after her nightmares.

She quickly opened the sheet of paper Crosby handed her; it was a birth certificate. "Tracy Terry" Diane read out loud. "...born March twenty-second nineteen eighty-eight." Diane closed the sheet of paper. She wasn't sure what to make out of this. Was this, Tracy her? She had the same birth date as her and it was also the name that was on most of the bonds in the garage.

Diane continued to read, mother, Jackie Terry, father unknown. Birthplace, Chicago. "Chicago" how did I get to Savannah Georgia, she thought. Why did I change my name to Diane? Was my life so bad that I needed to get away from my family and my name she thought? There were so many questions she needed answered. So many answers she was afraid of receiving.

"Are you ready?" Crosby asked with his hand extended. Diane reluctantly placed her hand in his. And just as she expected, the warmth was just as inviting as a hug from an old friend.

"I don't think I can be alone tonight.

Crosby laughed and looked at his watch. "You mean this morning." He laughed again bringing a smile to Diane's face. "I can work that out for you."

"It's morning!" Pamela's cheery voice rang out, as she opened the curtains to expose the Miami sun. She loved days like this; no plans no alarm clocks and no plans to return to Savannah. Her apartment back home was nice but this one was speechless. This apartment was what high society called a "smart house." Everything was automatic if you wanted. She had a washer and dryer, stainless steel appliance, and a top of the line vacuum. Not that she'd be using any of that stuff but it was nice to have them available.

The bedroom balcony opened up onto the beach and nothing can beat that. As long as Thomas and her dad stayed in business and that stupid wife of his remains unstable, she was set for life. Never- the-less, plan B was already in play; the money she acquired would serve her at least a few years in Spain and the rest of the money... well, she was certain that it would fall through also.

Even though she knew Thomas hated the smell of the ocean in the morning, Pamela threw the French doors open to let the sound of the Ocean waves take over the room. He'd been there with her for two days and now it was time for him to go. She wanted to enjoy the rest of the weekend without complaints and rules and all that other stuff Thomas does to get on her nerves. She didn't know how his wife could put up with him on a daily bases. Pamela shivered at the thought.

"Close those damn curtains" Thomas mumbled from under the pillows. Pamela smirked and went into the bathroom.

"What'd you say honey? I couldn't hear you over the tides" she laughed. She heard Thomas's heavy footsteps marching to the window, the French doors slamming shut and the curtains sliding closed. Pamela knew he'd march in to scold her next so she turned on the Boss radio on the shower wall and started singing and snapping her fingers. Thomas paused then marched straight to the kitchen. Pamela knew in a matter of hours- maybe four- she'd be alone to do whatever she wanted to do. She began to fill the tub for her two hour bath. He hated that too; how she would refill the tub over and over.

I'm tired of you too, Thomas thought as he waited for the agent to clear his card for a first class flight back to Georgia. He understood Pamela just as well as she understood him. Thomas knew she wanted to be in Miami alone, before they left Savannah but he wanted to come with her one last time. He was tired of the games and he knew that that detective would soon find out more than he wanted him to know. Even though his receptionist, Mary, said that no one had been there, he could always sense an unwanted presence. So as soon as he returned to Savannah, Judge McAfee, Pamela's father, would be his first disassociation.

Pamela was a nice enough girl but they don't make young girls like they used to. She's sassy, way too cheery and hard to tame, not like Diane. Diane was eager to learn and to be told what to do, and she was appreciative when he disciplined her roughness. Happy to not have to beg for cash at the gas station he pulled her from, she was damn near easy. Her having amnesia has been really hard on him. He's been too busy to re-train her and he damn sure wasn't going to replace her with Pamela. He shivered at the thought. I'll just have to spend some quality time with Diane and maybe she'll want to do some of the things he taught her to do over the years.

"What did you say?" Thomas was so deep in thought; he thought he heard the woman on the line say...

"Your card was declined sir" she said clearly. "I tried it twice" she announced before he could request that she'd try it again. "Do you have another card, Sir?" She was almost condescending but Thomas didn't have time for her nonsense. He had to get back to Georgia to see what damage Diane had done. If she closed the account then he was sure she was trying to move the bonds as well. Thomas read off the credit card numbers to his private account and wondered what Diane was doing with all that money. Had her memory come back? Was she planning on leaving him? Thomas couldn't decide what to think.

He got his confirmation number, dressed and took a cab to the airport. No luggage, no goodbyes. He'd send for his things later and Pamela, well, she'd get the picture. He tried to call his receptionist to no avail and his driver's phone kept going straight to voice mail. "What's going on" he said out loud. After trying to call his driver for the fourth time, he decided to leave a message to be picked up. He then called the bank and almost dropped his phone on the walking conveyor belt when the associate returned to the call.

"So she just withdrew all the money, she didn't make any purchases?" Thomas was shouting through the airport. Two hundred thousand dollars was far less than he had in his other accounts but for Diane to just take it without permission; his wrath was something even her amnesia couldn't save her from.

Crosby hated listening to the morning news. All bad news first thing in the morning was a sure fire way to put society in a negative mood. Hearing about hatred, distrust and dishonesty wasn't going to make people say "have a great day". However, listening to the news was a part of his job. The media knew more than the actual victims sometimes and even their false leads was a good way to seek out potential cases or suspects. That was the problem with his first case; he did not take the daily news into account, his arrogance fooled him into believing that he could find information on his own. Publicly shaking down suspects; running away possible witnesses, led to a kidnapped girl turning up dead. The young lady's life is something he will always charge himself with. Carelessness and unnecessary ego boosting will never be a factor in solving a case.

"What is she doing here?" Crosby asked out loud. He'd been staking out the Crawford's place since he dropped Diane at his secret hideout. Crosby was just about to stretch his numbing legs for the third time when the black Mercedes, K40-2598, Pamela hopped into pulled in front of him. He watched in anticipation for those long silky legs to fold out of the back seat but all was steel.

After a moment or two, the driver, Greg Young, Thomas Crawford's driver, slowly emerged. Crosby knew whomever Pamela was seeing was wealthy but he never would have guessed someone so closely knitted with her dad, Judge McAfee, whom he'd recently found in his search, was a frequent visitor to Thomas's office. Maybe she didn't know of their relationship he thought. But how could she not know. Did Diane know? Was that the purpose of her attack, she'd found something that she shouldn't have?

Crosby tried to untangle the information in his head as he watched the driver stand there staring at the Crawford's house as if waiting for someone to come running into his arms. Greg stepped from the side of the car and onto the driveway but then he suddenly noticed Crosby sitting there, pulled his cap down onto his forehead and ducked back into the car. The large man sat there for a moment before starting the engine.

Maybe he was waiting to see if Crosby would approach him or perhaps in his favor-leave first so that he may continue his stalking. Greg Young finally broke the silence by starting his engine and driving away leaving Crosby foggy but clear and alert at the same time.

Diane stretched her full-figured body along the strange bed she was lying on and regretted every move. The lent balls, which take years or hundreds of washes to develop, scraped across her bare legs like sand paper. "These sheets couldn't be no more than a two hundred thread count" she thought. She stretched again against her better judgment because over all, the full sized bed was comfortable. Then suddenly, as quick as a pesky gnat could invade your nose, so did a familiar aroma indulge Diane's. Although she has smelled brewed coffee a million times or more, this was different; this was someone's granny coffee.

Diane remembered waking up to that aroma and her Uncle Mike's alarm clock every morning, with him pushing the snooze button every ten minutes for a whole hour. She remembers getting angry at the stupidity of it all until the aroma of Folgers coffee, bacon and toast would sooth her just as quickly as the alarm annoyed her. Diane smiled at the fact, that at least once in her life time, she had a granny, somewhere who loved her.

Diane sat up and looked around the room. She took in a deep breath and smiled. With all the dollies on the dresser and book cases, she was expecting to smell molt balls or cat litter or something but the room smelled of lilac and Stetson cologne.

"Do you want something to eat sugar?" an elderly lady, wearing a crisp floral smock, stood in the doorway.

"Good morning. Yes I would ma'am." The lady put her hand on her hip.

"Well it isn't going to come to you" she smiled. "You'll find everything you need in the bathroom closet to freshen up and the kitchen is down the hall." She smiled again and 'sashayed' down the hall. Diane smiled at the kind aura the lady left behind. She was indeed, someone's Grannie. Well preserved too, like pressed flowers inside a favorite book; everything still in tack.

The halls and bathroom smelled of Caress soap, not all of the new perfumed ones, but the original pink one. Diane was surprised to find Aqua Fresh toothpaste; she didn't think anyone used that anymore. The living room surprised her even more. The sofa still had its original plastic covering on it, the kind that sits neatly around each pillow cushion. The tables were of that good old fashion wood, Diane was sure she used pure lemon oil and wiped in circles when she polished them.

The kitchen had a simple elegance about it; a few drawings of patrons dining 'al fresco', in Paris maybe, a coffee mug drawn by a child with crayons and a sign that read "Polly Anne's kitchen" Hung neatly on the wall. There were a few mugs hanging on hooks above the sink and everything had a pine fresh and clean scent. Ms. Polly moved gracefully throughout the kitchen as if age had yet to meet her. Her skin was tight and her gray hairs were few. Her arms were strong like she'd beat many behinds in her day, again, well preserved Diane thought.

As she sipped her coffee and waited for crisp bacon and toast to be placed in front of her, Diane thought of her Grannie. She tried to picture her face, her smell, her kindness and even the strength in her eyes but everything was vague.

"Terrance tells me that you've lost your memory." Although it was more of a statement then a question, she waited for Diane to answer.

"Yes, ma'am, that's true." Diane's stomach grumbled for the eggs and grits, she wasn't expecting, that was placed in front of her. The lady sat down across from her with a boiled egg inside an egg cup, and a coffee mug that read "grannies do it too". Sound like something you'd find in a Vegas gift shop.

"Have you been to Vegas?" Diane couldn't help but to ask. The lady looked at the mug then back at Diane.

"Ooh child! Yes! But that was in my younger years. Don't try to change the subject now."

"Yes ma'am, sorry"

"Anyway..." she went on. "Well the way I see it, and I see pretty clearly, people only remember what they want to remember."

"I do want to remember."

"Well maybe it's something you shouldn't remember." She sipped her coffee as she eyed Diane's wedding ring. "What does your husband say about all this?"

"He doesn't have much to say about it. He keeps telling me to leave it alone but how can I leave a lost past alone.

"Well maybe he..."

"Good morning, good morning, good morning ladies." Crosby walked into the kitchen vibrant and loud, purposely interrupting his granny.

"Boy what did I tell you about all that noise so early in the morning?" He leaned in to kiss her forehead and sat in the chair next to Diane.

"You said don't make it. How'd you sleep?" he winked at Diane.

"Did you know that her 'husband' has nothing much to say about her memory lost?" Crosby granny peered at him, Crosby didn't respond. He continued to look at Diane awaiting her response.

"Uh... yes I did. Thank you."

"Well I guess me and my breakfast will excuse ourselves into the den. If anybody needs us, just call." Crosby's granny grabbed her coffee mug and a newspaper from the table and quietly walked out.

"She's cute." Diane laughed

"Very." Crosby sat back in his chair and looked at Diane. She was pretty in the morning he thought. No makeup, just a nice clean face. "I could wake up to that face every morning" he thought.

"So I was thinking that maybe you could take me by my old apartment and..."

"Are you sure you want to do that?" Crosby was hoping she'd want to but he didn't want to be the one to give her the idea. Something he'd read online said that pressure could only suppress the memory even more. Diane didn't answer. Crosby stood to remove his coat, walked to the refrigerator and opened it.

"The juice is over to the left" Ms. Polly called out.

"How did she know" Diane laughed.

"She always knows" he laughed with her. After pouring his drink Crosby studied Diane, trying to see if she was strong enough for his questions. She seemed pretty focused and even determined since he gave her that copy of a birth certificate.

"Does the name Greg Young ring a bell?" he paused. "Or the name Pamela McAfee?" Diane stopped eating and thought for a minute.

"Greg Young defiantly sounds familiar," Crosby chest tightened for some reason. "He's Thomas's driver, I know that but Pamela doesn't ring a bell." Crosby relaxed a bit. It was a strange feeling but for some reason it bothered him to think that Diane and the driver had an affair. However, knowing that Pamela and Thomas were sneaking around didn't bother him at all.

"McAfee is the name of that Judge from the banquet." Diane swallowed the lump that instantly formed in her throat. Just saying the name suddenly made her nervous. "Judge McAfee" she said almost to herself. "I saw him on a photo somewhere in the house, Thomas's office, I believe." She could picture his mustache, smell his cigar and even hear his bellowing laugh. How does she know him so well she thought?

"Your husband does business with him?" Crosby asked, wondering what was going through her head. Diane's cheeks were flushed and she was starting to look faint.

Diane closed her eyes and tried to focus. She visualized big cases of money, an ash tray full of ashes and a room full of smoke. She could see herself standing nearby casually laughing at jokes only men would tell, serving them drinks.

"Oh God!" she sighed. What were her and Thomas into? Diane jumped up and paced the kitchen floor. She stopped and stared at Crosby. She wasn't looking at him but somehow through him. "Pamela's his daughter." Diane hated her. She hated her presence, her smile and the way her husband looked at her.

Diane remembered an argument she had with Pamela that changed a lot about how she viewed her husband.

"Stay away from Thomas" she'd told her.

"Tell Thomas to stay away from me". Pamela retorted, letting Diane know that her and Thomas's feelings for each other were mutual.

Just that quick reflection brought back many feelings for Diane. She remembered feeling used, angry and revengeful. "Can you take me to my old apartment?" Diane's face was firm and her stance was unyielding. Crosby knew that if he didn't take her himself, she was going to get there on her own.

Crosby and the not so frail lady, who opened the door to Diane's old apartment, voices faded as Diane entered the kitchen. She stared at the four slice slot toaster on the granite counter top that she envisioned days before in her home, until the image of her wine rack appeared. She smiled remembering the taste of her favorite black berry wine that filled the rack. Next to it was a very expensive wine opening kit. Thomas and she argued on end about the price she paid for it but she never returned it.

Diane suddenly jumped at the sound of a door slamming; she didn't turn because she was unsure of the realty of it. She felt alive but in a different dimension.

"Why didn't you call me when he left?" a voiced roared in her head. Confused and clear at the same time, Diane knew what was happening. She turned towards the door to face her fate. Greg Young's frame filled the doorway. He asked again

"Why didn't you call me...?"

"Didn't you drive him to the airport?" Diane interrupted.

Crosby and the tenant looked at her strangely. "Are you ok?" Crosby asked but Diane didn't respond. Her face and body language seemed to have transformed into a new person.

"She's not here" the tenant said backing away from Diane, pulling Crosby with her to the other side of the table. "I've seen this before" she whispered. "I saw it on a show called 'out of body' or something or another."

"Can't we get her out of it? Or back into it or whatever?" Crosby was confused. The Diane he'd known had disappeared. Diane now seemed stronger and more confident leaning on the counter with her arms and legs crossed at the ankles. There was no smile at the corner of her mouth. The slight sparkle that was once in her eyes was gone, replaced by black stones.

"No, we have to let her work it out. We have to give her space." The tenant slowly shook her head as a tear fell to her cheek. After Crosby explained that Diane had amnesia and wanted to see the apartment to see if something could jar her memory, the tenant, Ms. Jacobs, was more than eager and hurried them inside to get started. "But I warn you, she may be a whole different person when she's done. Crosby griped the lady's hand in fear. Why was he afraid? What could she do to him? Or was that the case. Maybe he was afraid of what he didn't know. He was afraid of finding out what type of person she really was, or worse, not liking the real Diane Crosby.

Diane bounced from the counter. "How could you say that? I've never..." she rushed from the kitchen. "Come back Gregory, I'm not done."

Crosby tensed as they followed Diane from the kitchen to the living room. His acquisitions' was right, her and Greg had a personal relationship.

"Just tell me you're leaving him as planned". Diane heard Greg say.

"I'm leaving him. Is that better?" She paused then gave him an evil grin. "It's not like you have someplace better for me to go." She chuckled.

"See why you have to be like that. You can't put a price on love Diane."

"You're right. So what's the plan Greg? Where are we going? What are we going to do for money?" Greg said nothing. He knew she was just speaking out of nervousness. But she was right; he had no plans for them, he hadn't even told his wife about them. He was hoping Diane would take the reins, book some flights to some place far off and they'd just leave.

"I thought so." Diane turned and headed towards the bedroom.

Crosby and the tenant waited as if to let Greg go before them. They slowly entered the bedroom almost expecting a hair brush or shoe to fly their way.

Greg grabbed Diane's arm and turned her towards him. She softened.

"Why are you doing this? Things would be much easier staying the way they are." Diane pleaded as Greg leaned his forehead on hers. The tingles she was getting as he rubbed his hands up and down her arms, almost made her forget what she'd be giving up if she ran away with him, almost.

"Oh, is this part of the plan Greg?" Pamela's sultry voice slammed into the room as the door banged against the wall. Diane jumped but not from fear. She was more annoyed with her presence than scared of her. She sometimes wished for the opportunity to pull her weave out, leaving her crawling on the ground for the pieces.

"Pamela, what are you doing here?" Diane sat on her bed and calmly put on her jewelry.

"Let me handle this" Greg tried to sound stern, but inside, his heart was aching and his stomach was turning.

"Hell no!" Pamela shouted, pushing Greg to the side. "You've already proved that you can't handle a damn thing and you've wasted enough time getting the wrong account number; as if two hundred grand would be enough for me."

"Greg, what is this? Pamela I have nothing to say to you." Pamela slapped the watch from Diane's arm. Diane jumped up from the bed and swung her arm to slap Pamela but was pushed back down by Greg. In shock, Diane looked from Pamela to Greg and back to Pamela.

"Now, Mrs. Thomas Crawford, we need a little old pin number and we'll...leave you alone."

"What?" Diane couldn't believe that this was a robbery. "Greg! Are you serious; the two of you are robbing me?" She shouted.

"Just give her the pin number baby and..." He was about to sit on the bed next to her but he was stopped by the glare in Pamela's eyes. "Just give us the pin to the master account and we'll leave, peacefully." Greg said that as more of a question to Pamela than a statement to Diane.

"I'm not giving you a damn thing" Diane crossed her arms. Pamela smacked her lips and pulled out a .22 from the back of her pants and for a fraction of a second Diane wanted to laugh but the cold steel against her forehead stifled that thought.

"Oh wow! Is this what it takes to shut you up? Pamela smiled then kissed the gun with intimacy, while watching Gregory. Their eyes locked for a moment and Pamela nodded towards Diane. Greg shook his head in defiance, sat on the bed next to Diane and then looked down at the floor. *"You little punk"* she shouted. She then smiled again and pointed the gun back to Diane. *"How cute. You're actually in love with her."* Pamela looked at the both of them then stood in front of Greg. She traced his lips with the gun as she parted his legs with her knees.

"Do you love her when I'm doing this?" She kissed him. Diane looked up to see if he kissed her back. He did. *"Does this look like love to you Diane?"* She forced Greg to look at Diane. Gregory's eyes were closed as if he was squeezing back tears.

"You're such a coward" Diane yelled at him. Greg eyes popped open. *"You can't run your household, you can't run me and you're not even in control of this so called robbery."*

"Shut up!" Greg stood up.

"Make me, little man." Diane tried to push past him and Pamela but Greg slapped her back down to the bed. She kicked him in the leg and Greg punched her in the stomach.

"Is that better?" He said between tears and fear.

"Finish her off Greg. We'll make Thomas give us the number."

Greg watched Diane as she fell to the floor on her knees crying. *"Do you love me?"* He asked holding her chin up to him. Diane looked at him and remembered all the lonely nights he filled in her bed, the happiness she felt from him that she never felt with Thomas and smiled.

"I've never loved you. You're weak and..." Greg didn't wait to hear the rest. He balled his fist up as Pamela laughed from behind him. The first hit was all Diane remembered.

Crosby watched as Diane's breathing came to a normal pace. She had been sitting on the edge of the bed for an hour it seemed. He wanted to shake her and save her from her thoughts but he knew that it was important for her to remember that night, no matter how painful it would be.

"Take me home" she said, but she didn't move. Crosby sat on the bed next to Diane and she looked at him as if it were the first time.

"Do you want to talk about it? What happened that night?"

Diane said nothing. She just looked through Crosby as she did the strangers through her mesh veil on her wedding day. On the ride back to her house, Diane hummed a song so evil, maybe from the phantom of the opera tainting Crosby's thoughts of her and he didn't want to see her this way.

"He was so nice when we first met." Diane said as a matter of fact.

"Greg was nice?" Crosby didn't know what Diane was about to say next but he wasn't prepared to hear about her and Greg's affair.

"Thomas was nice. I should have known better. The only true lesson my mother taught me was that good things don't come easy." Crosby sat quietly, not wanting to interrupt her, now that she was beginning to talk. "I used to pump gas at the gas station for change" she continued. "The first time that I saw Thomas, he was dressed in a white linen suit and he wouldn't let me pump his gas." Diane chuckled. "In fact, he never did. At first he would show up once a week, then every day and then eventually he started dropping twenty dollar bills in my hand. But he didn't let me pump his gas. He then began to pull me to the side and talk to me for hours, the gifts started coming shortly after that." Diane laughed loudly in amusement. "It's funny, if I think about it, Thomas actually courted me."

"Sounds like it." Crosby was amazed. He would have never placed Diane in a bad place. She looks and acts as if she was born in this high class life. "So, is your real name, Tracy?"

"Yes."

"Why did you change it? Why did the two of you move to Savannah? Does your family...?" Crosby noticed Diane's hands ringing together so he stopped his questioning. He was pressuring her, so now it was time to pull back before he lost her all together. "Just relax; you've been through a lot today." He reached over to pat the back of her hand and she nervously moved her hand away.

"Do you want to know why I left home?" Diane continued as if Crosby hadn't said a word. "One night after the many dinners Thomas took me to, making me feel like a queen, I over slept and came home the next morning. I was so afraid that my mother was up all night worrying about me; my heart was racing so fast that it was hard for me to breathe. I opened the door to find my mother sitting at our second hand store kitchen table, drinking coffee without a care in the world. She might have well stabbed me in my heart because what she said to me that morning was far worse. Without even looking up from her cup, she said "I hope that coochie made me some money last night". I wanted to die right there in her kitchen floor. Who says such things to their daughter?" Diane paused. "So every time I brought money into the house she thought that it was from prostituting. I was a virgin until Thomas and I got married and she will never know it."

"You never told her the truth?" Diane didn't answer Crosby's question, she just stared out of the window as he drove. When they pulled into the driveway, Diane's whole demeanor had changed.

"Thank you so much officer." She smiled. "I'll be in touch." She quickly got out of the car.

"Um... can you come down to the precinct and file a report?" Diane slammed the door and peered through the window.

"I'll be in touch" she said again with a smirk a mother would have given to let her child know that she will not keep repeating herself. Crosby knew that he had the power to make her come in but felt that she had been through enough for one day. He nodded a yes as she turned away. She was different, cold and distant. Diane was no longer vulnerable and Crosby feared her actions. He had to stay close and alert for her sake. And for Greg Young, should he choose to come back.

Where was Pamela he thought? His informant told him Thomas left Miami alone, a day ago but no one has seen him in Savanna. What were Pamela and Greg after? It had to be more than money if Pamela wanted it. It was time to close this case before someone got seriously hurt.

Thomas woke to the sound of traffic rolling by his head. He spat out some blood that was trying to seep down his throat just as a driver, on her cell phone, swerved her car from hitting him. He slowly rose and made his way up the hill from the highway feeling horrible. He wished Judge McAfee's men had killed him instead of making him go through the pain he was now feeling. Not only did he have broken ribs and a broken nose, he also had... he looked at the empty place on his wrist, a place that used to hold his watch, it was gone. When he was dumped under the viaduct, he was told that he had twelve hours to produce the bonds from the laundered money. Not knowing how long he'd been knocked out, he was now desperate for the time.

Thomas ducked into a nearby diner and headed toward the men's room. His reflection in the mirror looked worse than what he felt. His eye was swollen, his nose was bent and blood was all over his yellow Gucci shirt. "That fat no good uncle tom, no neck, never getting laid... Judge McAfee had a lot of nerve" he thought. He'd made him millions on top of millions of dollars and this is the gratitude he receives, to leave him beaten and broke.

He painfully wiped the blood from his face as he waited for Greg, who's only excuse for not picking him up from the airport-leaving him open for this torment-was that he didn't get the call. He'd have to check him later on that, but for right now, Greg was the only one he could trust.

By the time Greg arrived with a fresh shirt and bandages for Thomas, he'd only had four hours to produce the bonds that he worked hard for; the very bonds he was looking forward to spending alone since Diane had amnesia and Pamela chose to throw away her opportunity when she threw out their relationship. The bonds that were now missing from the empty tool box he was now staring into in his garage.

"I thought I told you to watch the house?"

"I did" Greg responded startled. He watched every movement in and out of that house. He watched Diane get dressed, undress, eat and sleep. He even watched, with heartache, when Diane broke down and lost control on her neighbor's front yard a few days ago. He wanted so badly to hold her and tell her that everything would be alright. He never told Thomas about the detective hanging around either. He didn't want Thomas to hear the guilt in his voice. Why didn't he leave after Diane went into her coma? What did he have to gain by risking everything? He and Pamela both had plenty to lose but he wasn't smart enough to leave. Maybe he truly loved Diane and was afraid to leave her alone not knowing if she'd be ok.

"Who is that" Thomas asked desperately. Greg stepped to the garage window just in time to see Diane leaning into the detective's car window. Thomas pushed Greg from the window but carefully holding onto him all the same. "I've seen that car before." He paused. Greg didn't respond. They waited for Crosby to drive away before they headed into the house.

Diane rushed into the house and slammed the door behind her. She leaned against the door until Crosby drove away. When she couldn't hear the car tires anymore, she sunk down to the floor and cried. She remembered the whole day of her accident. She and Thomas argued that morning on his way to Miami, her mother called asking for more money and Greg had asked her to marry him. She loved Greg and now felt a deeper pain knowing, now, that he was responsible for putting her into a coma. She turned down his proposal but she didn't break it off with him. There was too much to lose for the price of love; she had that business with Judge McAfee, Thomas still had to be dealt with and she still needed to transfer more bonds.

Diane jumped up remembering the bonds in the garage, and ran towards the kitchen. She stopped short just as Thomas and Greg walked through the door to the garage. There seemed to be a long pause between the three of them. Diane couldn't believe Greg had the audacity to still be in town, let alone in her house after all that he's done.

Greg was unsure of Diane's memory and Thomas was certain that her amnesia was swinging hand and hand with his bonds all the way to Switzerland.

"Where are the bonds Diane?" Thomas reached for her holding his ribs, but Diane dodged him stepping to the other side of the kitchen.

"What are you talking about" she tried to sound clueless. Greg didn't make a move. He just stood there looking weak.

"You know damn well what I'm talking about." Thomas reached for a chair and Greg helped him to sit. Diane stood there with her arms crossed tapping her foot on the floor tile, scanning the room for a weapon. The cutlery set was on the counter behind Greg but the rolling pin was in the utensil bowl just a few feet from her reach and by the way the color was fading from Thomas's face, she knew she could get to it before he got to her.

How will she handle this she thought? She's blocked by someone who tried to kill her and another who would kill her to get his way. "I don't have time for this, bring her to me" Thomas ordered Greg. At first he hesitated but then Greg began to cross the room. It was something about the way Greg moved that told Diane that he didn't want to hurt her, so at that moment she decided to pit Thomas against Greg. As Greg got closer Diane started to inch away, whimpering while tears rolled down her face. Greg stopped in his tracks and looked at Thomas.

"Please don't beat me again" she shouted.

"What!" Thomas yelled and slowly rose from his chair.

"I'll give you and Pamela the pin numbers, I promise Greg, just don't put me in a coma again." Diane let out a swill cry and coward into the corner of the kitchen. And just as she thought, more like hoped, Thomas charged at Greg with all the strength that he had. Greg, confused and caught off guard, was pushed into the refrigerator with a thud. Feeling guilty and the need to be punished, Greg didn't fight back. He kept his eyes on Diane while Thomas punched and kicked him.

Reluctantly, Diane closed her eyes as she listened to the grunts and moans of two men she had once loved. She can almost forgive Gregory for being weak and turning against her. She had falsely promised him a new life with her, with money beyond measure, so what else was he to do out of desperation. She had no other choice but to have the bonds changed over to her name-the benefits of a joint bank account-and leaving evidence to prove that Thomas was stealing from the Judge, was harder than she thought but by the looks of Thomas's face, proved affective.

Neither one of those bastards deserved anything but jail time. Judge McAfee was as dirty as they come, sentencing the innocent for popularity and freeing the guilty for cash. And Thomas's beatings were wearing her thin. So what he found her on the street, struggling, created a new identity and a life for her. Nothing gives him the right to hit her at will.

"You dirty little whore." Thomas shouted, grabbing her by the hair. "Were you screwing him?" Thomas pulled her to her feet and spat in her face.

"You're a weak excuse for a man." Diane tried to break free. "Is that all you got?"

"Slut" Thomas said throwing Diane back down to the floor. "Where're the bonds? I know you hid them."

"I don't know what you're talking about" Diane shouted trying to get out of Thomas's reach. Thomas straddled her placing his knees against her arms and slapping her. Just as he raised his fist to strike her again, Diane heard the kitchen table turn over and she felt Thomas weight being lifted off of her. Greg had pulled Thomas up by his neck and threw him down on his back. He began kicking at Thomas's broken ribs while Thomas tried desperately to grab hold to Greg's feet.

"Get the hell out of here!" Greg yelled at Diane. Diane hesitated for a moment but the look on Greg's face told her that he wasn't taking no for an answer. Greg reached behind him and pulled out a .9mm-his best friend since Judge McAfee's men made him leave the airport-and aimed it at Thomas's head.

"Greg, he's not worth all of that" Diane screamed backing out of the kitchen. "Let's just go. Leave him!" she cried.

"No, someone needs to teach him a lesson" Greg's words were as hard and definite as his fist when they harshly kissed Diane's face a few months ago.

"And who's going to teach him, you?" Diane's truth hit Greg like a ton of bricks, slamming down on his head, leaving him for dead. She was right. Here he was trying to punish Thomas for doing the same thing that he'd done. The very thing he wanted his love for her to erase from her memory. Giving in to Pamela's threats to include him into the money laundering was easier than excepting Diane's rejection to marry him, so he used it as justification for leaving her in a coma. Maybe he was trying to kill her. Or kill the fact that he couldn't have her, relieving her of the pain Thomas caused and relieving himself of the guilt of loving her.

He will never forgive himself. Not even the two million dollars Pamela promised, could wipe away the blood on his hands. Greg kneeled down closer to Thomas, held the gun to his head and closed his eyes. In his mind he pulled the trigger, blood splattered and Thomas was dead. Diane cried tears of joy and they walked off into the sunset. However, reality was taking place all around him. When Greg opened his eyes, the gun barrels of three police officers were pointed at him, Thomas was trying effortlessly to raise his hands and Diane was crying insanely into the bosom of Detective Crosby. Would she tell him everything Greg wondered? He tried to read Diane's face as he was pulled to his feet. He looked for a wink or some hint from her that today's event would be her only story, but Diane didn't look at him or at anyone for that matter. She kept her innocent little head buried into the detective's jacket.

Crosby read Gregory Young and Thomas Crawford their rights as the officers cuffed the bleeding men. He made sure their memorandums were done properly because unlike his first case, this one would not be thrown out on a technicality. He knew he'd get an accommodation for this one. Thomas's secretary was a tremendous help; due to his rudeness over the years, she was happy to tell him about all the visits that Judge

McAfee paid to the office and she made sure to show him the fluctuating balances in the company's ledger.

After putting two and two and three together, Crosby figured out the money laundering scheme between Thomas and the Judge, and Thomas's affair with Pamela, stung him a little because it went all the way back to when they were engaged. Greg's and Pamela's attack on Diane was surprising and the affair between she and Greg, was something he didn't want to believe. He didn't believe it until Diane had said so herself.

He looked down at Diane as she sat in one of the plush kitchen chairs. Her sobs subsided as the men in her life were lead out to the perspective squad cars waiting for them. Could she be as innocent as she tried to appear he thought? The very thought he was having when he spotted Greg Young's car two blocks over without a driver in it. Not once did he see her name on anything concerning the Crawford's business. Not even on delivery sheets.

It was strange considering that the secretary mentioned that Diane sat in on all the meetings with the Judge and that she ordered her around just as much as Thomas did. However he had nothing to tie her to the money, and what was said in the meeting was only speculation, therefore there was nothing to charge her with. He'd have to get a warrant to thoroughly search the property for more evidence and to find the actual bonds.

"Diane, I know that you're feeling pretty bad right now but I need to bring you in to make a statement at this time." Diane heard Crosby say, bringing her back to reality. Her mind was focused on what her story would actually be. She looked at Crosby for a moment then rose up and walked to the French doors. Her complexion was pale but she still looked alive. Even through her reflection, she could see that the scar Thomas left behind would soon be gone. She smiled at the thought of that having a double meaning. She saw Crosby's reflection looking worried as he tried to patiently wait for her response. Diane knew he was aware of her attackers now and since he didn't arrest her, she also knew that he hadn't connected her to the money yet. She wasn't sure if he knew about the bonds or what really went on in the kitchen but she knew that she owed him an explanation of some sort.

"Can you give me a couple of minutes to freshen up and I'll be right out." Diane said without waiting for a response. She hurried past Crosby to her bedroom then waited a few seconds to make sure that he hadn't followed her. She heard the back door close and exhaled. As quickly as she could, Diane ran to the garage, pulled out some of the bonds from the lawn mower and looked at them. They read "to the order of Tracy Terry". Diane held back tears of joy as she carefully stuffed them back inside the lawn mower bag. Diane closed her eyes and said a quick prayer, hoping some smart ass cop, if granted a warrant today, would just figure it was grass and leaves inside and don't insist on opening the bag.

Diane dusted off her knees and wiped her face with her t-shirt. Her jaw hurt like hell but fifty million dollars in bonds could buy her a new one. She slowly walked towards Crosby's car glancing toward the squad cars that held her lovers. Her lovers, in which she would tell, were fighting over Greg's involvement of her attack that led to her coma and amnesia. If one of them, Greg or Thomas, chose to mention the bonds, she would deny it until death. She worked hard for that money and she'd put up with a lot of Thomas's abuse. From the moment she met him while begging for money in a gas station in Chicago, to grinning through political meetings and ten thousand dollars a plate dinners, Diane deserved every crumpled up bond that waited for her.

She winked at Thomas as he sneered at her through the window. Greg on the other hand looked miserable beyond measure. His sadness actually stopped Diane in her tracks and her knees almost buckled when she read his lips saying that he was sorry. Diane sat quietly as Crosby called in favors to friends in Miami. He wanted immediate information on Pamela's whereabouts. Even though he hadn't found the bonds he heard Thomas speak of yet, he now had enough to at least arrest Pamela, along with Greg for their attempted murder.

Diane actually hoped they wouldn't find her. Confronting her on her betrayal would be more than exciting. Having Greg beat her was part of the plan but leaving her in a coma wasn't. Pamela wasn't even supposed to show up; Diane was going to taunt Greg into hitting her, to receive the scares that she needed, wreck Thomas's office and the garage, break the lock on the tool box, hide the bonds and then tell the police that it was a robbery and Greg beat her until she gave up the PIN code to their bank account, in which she had already transferred the money. However, Pamela double crossed her, so instead of planting seeds in her father that Thomas was stealing from him, she was making provisions to keep the money herself and now Diane needed a plan to pay her back for her efforts. Diane's fist balled up thinking about it. Crosby grabbed her hand and rubbed her fist away. She relaxed under his touch and he was pleased.

He wished that this moment could last longer but he knew that he may never see her again. She'd probably go to Chicago, reunite with her family and try to forget her days here in Savanna; she had no reason to stay here. Maybe if she knew that it was he that sat with her every night that she was in the hospital, prayed for her, and read scriptures until his voice cracked, she would then have a reason. She would then know that someone loved and wanted to protect her but this, she'll never know.

Diane will begin another journey in less than a week and may only think of him once or twice before the year was out. No matter the outcome, Crosby was glad to have met such a strong woman. His time with her during her coma opened up his heart again, releasing some past hurt and allowed him to trust again.

THE END

BORROWED LOVE

BORROW;

To acquire temporarily with the promise or intentions of returning.

Throughout life we find ourselves in and out of love and relationships. Some last for months or even years. And there are some that last for days. A relationship deals with the sharing of time, common interest and of one self. And if we step outside of that relationship, we give of ourselves, when we don't always belong to ourselves causing the person that we are seeing to borrow love from our significant other. How so? Take marriage for example; the wife belongs to the husband and the husband belongs to the wife. Are they borrowing? No, you are. When you date a married man or woman you are borrowing from their spouse with the intentions of returning him or her. Depending on how long you're in that relationship...

Kemiece had heard enough, the relationship specialist on the radio was getting on her last nerve. She walked over to the radio mounted under her kitchen cabinet and harshly pressed the off button. How can you borrow something without the other person knowing? That just doesn't make any since. If anything the woman or the man is lending out "stuff" that don't belong to them and the innocent person, in the middle, like herself gets hurt in the process. She slammed her rubber gloved hand down on the counter cluttered with the cabinet's contents.

When she was angry or really worried, Kemiece would clean her apartment from front to back and at this moment she was both worried and angry. Kemiece cleaned aimlessly around her apartment while she examined her past weeks and questioned her relationship of three years, with John. The more she thought the more the walls seemed to be coming down all around her and her head seemed to be spinning out of control. The clock was ticking extra loud and her vision was getting blurred. "I have to get out of here" she spoke out to the whirlwind around her.

Kemiece grabbed her purse and her keys and bolted out the door. Paying no attention to the paint splashed jeans and the faded t-shirt she was wearing. Not to mention the run over flip-flops, flapping against her feet. Never-the-less, Kemiece drove full force to Sister's house, hoping to get pulled over for a speeding ticket to justify the anger that she was feeling, to put forth blame for her attitude and to divert her attention, just for a little while, to something else. How could she be so stupid, so blind to the phony gestures and smiles? So easy to believe everything that he said; "I appreciate you" and "you're everything to me" are things he should have kept to himself. Sister would have figured it out before the breath escaped his lips.

Sister was her "ace boom coon", her best friend, her confidant, and her truth when she was faced with lies and her rhyme when she had no reasoning. Sister was the stronger version of herself... Kemiece thought about that for a minute, she didn't feel strong at all when she compared herself to her sister. Sister could tell a person where to get off in such a way that they would thank her for her honesty and still want to be around her. Kemiece, on the other hand had the ability to express her feelings but never to the actual person, only to Sister. Sister was uninhibited and that made her the perfect person to vent to.

Funny thing about venting your problems out to someone, you can't control what they will say, when they say it or even how they say it. All you can do is take it or leave it. And if you decide to leave it, do you actually leave it? Words can become embedded in your soul; so much so that when you think that you're avoiding the speaker, to prevent another lecture, you're in turn remembering every word and sometimes inventing new words you believe they would say.

"You must be out of your mind! Ain't no way I'm going to be tormented by a love triangle with some man and his wife." Sister shook her dread-locked head in disgust as she pulled leaf after leaf from its collard green stem. She was getting a little tired of hearing about her little sister's problems, not that she didn't want to be there for her, but she was tired of hearing new problems from the same old man. "What you need is a free man."

"Sister you mean a single man" Kemiece spoke for the first time since she told her older sister that the man she'd been seeing for the past three years was married. Sister stopped picking greens and looked at Kemiece over the rim of her glasses.

"Kem, you ain't hearing me. I said free and I mean free." Kem waved her off and began to fill a pot with water. She couldn't remember the last time her sister even claimed to even know a man on a personal level, and here she was giving her advice about getting a free one. "It doesn't matter if I have a man or not. Right is right." Sister read her thoughts again. Kem could never hide anything from her sister, even when they were growing up. Kem remembered running to their parents screaming "Sister's a witch" after she'd guessed every color and number that she could think of.

"I'm serious girl. A single man is a man who just isn't married. It doesn't mean he doesn't have anybody, but a free man, he doesn't have anybody. He's free to do whatever, whenever and however. You got me?"

"I hear you." Surprisingly Kem understood what Sister was saying. She usually uses a lot of metaphors and parables to explain her thoughts. It would usually take Kem days to figure out her sister's theories, stories or whatever message she was trying to convey to her. "But how am I to know if they're married, and if I ask, how would I know that they're telling the truth? Take John for example; three years and wham!" Kem smacked her hand on the counter for more effect. "I'm hit over the head." Was there a sign before that horrible phone call? There had to have been a sign that John was married. Kem quickly retraced the past three years searching for a sign of some sort. She found nothing.

Did John make her that happy that his brief distances went unnoticed? Were her unanswered calls a figment of her imagination? Maybe she wasn't dreaming when John moaned out some other woman's name. There is always a sign and Kem had missed them all. The phone calls that were taken in another room, text messages instead of phoning her on his off days and always paying cash for everything from dinner to hotel rooms could have easily been overlooked because she was so understanding and not the typical jealous and insecure woman that her friends were.

"Girl, you're getting water all over my floor!" Sister was yelling as she jumped up from the table to get a mop. Kem turned the faucet off and grabbed some paper towels from the kitchen counter. "I can't believe you still daydream like when we were kids." Sister vigorously mopped the water from the floor ignoring her sister's poor attempt to clean with paper towels. "Hear me good Kemiece, you need a free man, that's it, that's all."

Kem left Sister's house feeling worse than she had when she rolled out of bed this morning. Everything seemed gray; the sky, her thirty-year-old hair seemed gray, her neighbors tan and white dog, who was taking a dump in their yard when she left this morning, even appeared to be gray. How could John be married Kem thought? All the time that they'd spent together was incredible. And what about their month-long vacations they took every year. Where was his wife then? Was she vacationing with the mailman?

How can a man do such a thing? More importantly, Kem thought, why wasn't she more upset about it? "I should be pissed off" she screamed at the rearview mirror as she drove home. The average woman would be home in a bathrobe hugging a pint of ice cream and a bag of cookies plotting revenge. Not Kem. In fact, Kem couldn't wait to see John again. There had to be a simple explanation. John is just too happy when he's with her. There has to be a simple explanation.

EXPLAIN;

Make clear or intelligible, say by way of explanation, account for one's conduct. Give an account of one's meaning, motives etc.

John paced the floor of the restaurant as he waited for Kemiece's arrival. His stomach was aching with anticipation not knowing what she would say about him being married. It was much too late when he had realized that it was Kemiece on the telephone the night of the accident. He had answered the phone so much in a panic, thinking that his sister was the caller, that he had blurted out "my wife is in the hospital and you're playing around not answering the phone." Kem hung the phone up without a word hoping and praying she'd dialed the wrong number. When she had called back all she said was "John". And when he had said "yes" Kem simply hung the phone up and they haven't spoken in a week. John emailed her to meet him at the restaurant, and he was hoping that this wouldn't be the one time that she didn't want to hear an explanation of his screw up.

John's heart skipped a beat when he turned towards the entrance to see Kem standing in the door. She seemed to be extra beautiful; her lips seemed fuller, her smile looked brighter, and her legs were longer. Maybe he missed her, John thought. Or maybe his fear of losing her enhanced her beauty.

"Hi sweetie" Kem smiled and gave John the warmest embrace he'd ever received from her. Not knowing that that was the hardest thing she ever had to do, embrace with love when feeling indifferent. John tried to read her thoughts before he spoke. He couldn't read that her eyes were throwing daggers at his head, or that her teeth were clenching and not smiling, so he just jumped right into the fire and hoped he didn't get burned too badly.

"I'm sorry you had to find out like that."

"Let's get a table first." Kem took his hand and gave it a tender squeeze. That way you could think of something better to say Kem thought. For the next half hour, as they waited for a table, they talked about everything other than themselves; the weather, politics, and even celebrities whom Kem hated to talk about but it was better than the conversation to come.

John was playing suck up, by buying everything in the restaurant souvenir shop that he thought Kem wanted. He even bought something for Sister, whom he knew would do her best to make Kem forget about him. He couldn't let Kem get away, he needed Kem in his life and that's the way it was going to be. After the food was ordered John wasted no time to save himself.

"Kemiece I didn't want you to leave me" John said with pleading eyes.

"Why didn't you give me that choice? I should be the one to decide if I want..." Kem thought about the radio program she heard days before... "borrowed love."

"I didn't want to take that chance, Kem. It was supposed to be over between me and my wife a long time ago, but..." John was searching for words that were as close to the truth as possible.

"But, what?"

"But the time just didn't seem right." John looked around the room to see if anybody was listening.

"What do you mean, the time wasn't right. The right time would have been on the night you told me you love me. Or how about on our first vacation together. Hell, in three years, the right time has come and gone a thousand times" Kem was furious now. Good she thought; I am normal. The waiter brought out their food which gave them both some time to take a deep breath.

"I didn't think that she could handle it," John said when they were alone again. Kem said nothing. "Kem, I met you when I thought my marriage was over and you made me forget all my problems. Then just as we were doing so well my wife started changing, 'acting right'." John fidgeted with his shrimp.

"So there's still hope for your marriage?" Kem didn't know what she wanted his answer to be. If he chose her would she be dismissed when she wasn't 'acting right'? Up to this point in their conversation, Kem had actually planned to sleep with him at least one more time... just to say goodbye but now that thought was so out of reach.

"Truthfully, I don't know." John slumped down in his seat and leaned his head back. At that very moment John had become the ugliest man in the world; his hands that used to touch her vulnerable parts ever so gently, looked like claws and his pores seemed to open up into holes large enough for his lies to fall deep into. John's perfectly white teeth, that nibbled on her ear lobes, were suddenly yellow and his smooth chocolate skin now formed pus-filled razor bumps. The smell of John's skin went from the Italian Musk he uses to just plain old musk. Kem grabbed her stomach in hope to ease nausea she now felt. How can she ever open her heart to him again? It was officially over between the two of them.

"John!" Kem called his name with clenched teeth. Like a parent trying not to yell at her child in public. John shot up as if he were that child.

"Yeah, baby." He responded with a hint of hope on his tongue.

"If and when you get a divorce and I don't mean filing for one but have completed signed papers in hand, give me a call." Kem stood up, adjusted her skirt and clutched her purse under her arm.

"That is if you can reach me."

As Kem pictured John's chin on the floor and his eyes on her untouched meal, she took out her cell phone and called her phone service to have her number changed. In exactly one month Kem's stern words to John meant absolutely nothing. After the first week, she began to miss his voice. When the second week rolled around, she found herself dialing his number and hanging up before it had a chance to ring. So naturally, at the end of the fourth week; their old pictures failed to satisfy her eyes, her lips longed to feel his and her body missed everything that he had ever done to her.

Kem found herself touching every place on her body that John has ever visited, just to put herself to sleep at night so when John showed up at her door step with flowers, a Barry White CD, some sparkling cider and a freshly toned body, which now again set off the aroma of Italian Musk with a touch of sandalwood, every wall that she erected was now weakening in the crevices of logic.

"I'm getting a divorce. We've already filed the papers and our lawyers are working on the details because of the house. Kem, I need you. Please don't give up on me yet." Didn't I say signed divorced papers Kem thought as she looked beyond John trying to catch a glimpse of her face in an imaginary mirror, to see if she looked like a fool?

You think you can just pop up here looking all good, smelling all good, licking those lips of yours, and your chest all puffed out and tight. Get away! Go home! I'm done with you! Kem willed herself to say these words out loud but all she could say was...

"Are you coming in?"

FILLER;

An item serving only to fill space or time, a person or thing that fills a space or container

"It's been about a month" Kem was confessing to Sister about her revived relationship with John. Kem had been lying about her whereabouts for weeks and they were beginning to topple onto one another so Sister demanded the truth.

"Hump" was all that Sister said after what seemed like an eternity had gone by. "Are you coming to my dinner party?" Kem felt horrible now, she knew by association, that if Sister suddenly changed subjects on you, that meant that she was done with the topic forever. And if she was done talking about her and John, she'd have to find someone else to confide in when the time came.

"Yes."

"Cool, if you find the time I would appreciate your help with the decorations." Sister's words felt cold as ice, even over the phone lines. Kem shivered at the thought of not being able to talk to Sister about any and everything under the sun. She knew that she was wrong, in a way, for continuing to see John before his divorce was final but she was so used to him being around that "this" just felt like her only alternative.

"You know that doesn't balance, right?" Stephanie was looking over Kem's shoulder shaking her head. Kem looked down at the budget she was balancing and shook her own head at the figures. "What's wrong with you today" Stephanie took the ledger from Kem and began to erase at the errors at the bottom of the page. She handed the book back to Kem and handed her another book with a note attached. Kem almost dropped the book seeing John's name on the note. "His wife must be a fast reader or a stay at home wife or something because he comes in every Sunday to pick up a new book."

"Wow, only on Sunday's huh. Does his wife ever come with him?" Kem tried to sound nonchalant, but she could even hear the nervous tremble in her voice.

"I've never seen her but he and his son are always too cute. I'll be back in thirty, ta ta." Stephanie left the store almost skipping and Kem's heart felt like it was skipping twelve beats at a time. Since she'd found out about John's wife, he'd stopped coming into the shop and now he's sneaking into her shop, on the only day that she didn't come into work, to keep up the "good husband" routine in the midst of a quote, unquote divorce. And to top it off, he has never mentioned having a son to her. Kem used to think that John kept his wife a secret because he didn't want to lose her but now... she feels as though John doesn't feel she's worthy. "Maybe he's a flat out liar" Sister's voice echoed in Kem's head.

Kem looked up just in time to see John's car pull up to the shop and stop. John got half way out of the car, looked over at Kem's car and then got back into his car and drove away. He's such a coward. Before John's car could get out to the main street, Kem's cell phone was ringing. The only reason she was in today was because he bailed on their date with the excuse of not feeling well so she figured he was calling to see how much of him, if any part, did she see. Kem didn't answer the phone.

Kem made it through the rest of that day without answering John's calls but by the time she got home, showered and fluffed her pillows for the night, she couldn't help but to answer the phone to hear what kind of excuse he would have this time.

"It's not an excuse, it's the truth." John's voice cracked. Kem secretly hoped he bit his tongue as well.

"And what's your truth for not telling me that you have a son..."

"I have a son, what else you want me to say?" John interrupted. "I don't need an excuse for having a child with my wife." John said "wife" in a way to tell her that what he does with "her" is none of her business, ever. In actuality, it wasn't any of her business and neither was she... supposed to be, his business. Kem guessed that by John's actions that she was just to appreciate the time that he gave her, space filler when his wife is unable or... something. Kem couldn't think of anything else.

She was just borrowing him for a time... there was that word again. "I'm sorry; I shouldn't have said it like that" John paused long enough for Kem to hear him breathing. She wanted to say something but the words that she was feeling was having a hard time reaching her lips. "I didn't tell you because I didn't want to confuse my son."

"How can telling me..."

"Because I know you were going to insist on meeting him and I'm not ready to do that" John cut her off again. Kem decided not to say anything at all, something else that Sister said more than once or twice; "Let a man do all the talking and you'll find out a lot about him". With all the relationship knowledge that Sister has given her, Kem couldn't believe how she ended up in this situation. She didn't have low self-esteem, as far as she was willing to admit and she definitely wasn't ugly so why was she accepting this treatment from this man who claims to love her? What had she done to let him know that this was ok?

FREE;

Not physically restrained, obstructed, or fixed; unimpeded.

The following week was an emotional headache for Kem, she even snapped at one of her regular customers who, to Kem's relief, dismissed it as Kem working too hard. "Sweetie you need to take it easy sometime" she said. And that was exactly what she and John had planned for the weekend. After a long emotional cry that they had together, she and John decided to fly to New York on Friday to grab dinner and a stage play and return on Sunday. "Had" being the operative word, now today was Saturday and Kem was leaving her third message of the day. "John, give me a call when you get this message." Fooled again by John's weeping eyes and sincere words of a future together, Kem felt like an idiot once again and she couldn't even call Sister to tell her about it. John called Friday morning to say he was going home to change from his workout attire and he'd call when he was on his way. Kem hasn't heard from him since.

The clock was about to strike nine and she was home alone, contemplating on binge eating a pint of Haagen-Dazs and some cookies when her phone began to ring. Kem dashed out of the kitchen, through the dining room and bumped her shoulder as she rounded the corner to her bedroom.

"Ouch! Hello." Kem shouted in pain as she answered the phone.

"My, my, my, is someone having a bad night." Sister sang out in a good mood.

"Hey Sister what's up?" Kem rubbed her shoulder as she examined herself in the mirror.

"What's wrong with you and what took you so long to answer the phone?"

"I had the phone on the charger and I was in the kitchen."

"Why can't you put a landline in the kitchen again? Oh yeah! You're never in the kitchen right. Isn't that what you said?" Sister was clearly amused.

"Okay you called because..." Kem was excited to hear from her sister but she was not in the mood for a lecture.

"Get dressed I want you to go somewhere with me."

"How do you know I haven't got plans?" Kem knew by her sister's silence, that Sister knew that John was nowhere to be found but she wouldn't dare say it. This was the third weekend in a row and this game was getting tired. John's first excuse was that his wife started an argument on his way out the door and he couldn't call because she snatched his cell phone and broke it. Go to a pay phone Kem thought or better yet drive over to my house; it's not like she wasn't expecting him.

His second reason didn't make sense at all; he went with his wife to his mother-n-law's birthday party... is that something divorcing couples would do. Something was telling Kem to wake up but she just couldn't feel the shoving, not just yet. But eating ice cream on a Saturday night wasn't something that she wanted to do either.

"I'll be ready in one minute." Kem laughed already feeling better.

"I'll give you forty-five minutes because you lie too much." Sister hung up laughing also.

The Chicago air was awesome; seventy five degrees on a summer night was as good as it gets. Lake Michigan smelled semi-clean, parents were letting their children burn off the last of their energy at the park and the neighbors walking their dogs looked more like a hobby than a chore in Hyde Park, Kem thought.

"Stop daydreaming and get in the car," Sister yelled.

"Sorry" Kem popped out of her trance and got in the car with a serene smile on her face.

"Man that must have been a good one." Sister made a U-turn from south to north right in front of an oncoming car.

"Girl, you still can't drive." Kem laughed holding on to the door handle.

"Sweetie, don't go changing the subject."

"Okay remember when I used to say that I'll marry the first man to buy me a dog."

"Yeah." Sister slammed on her brakes and turned to face her little sister. "Don't tell me John bought you a dog."

"No he didn't. I just remembered that's all. Now drive! You're holding up traffic."

"You cut your hair."

"Yes, now drive." Sister gave Kem another long look, smiled and then waved her apologies to the cars piling up behind her.

The 'Brown Sugar' club was in full effect when they arrived; the jazz was flowing into the parking lot and Kem couldn't wait to get inside. Her brand new jeans were calling for attention, not to mention the new hair cut she got earlier that day; a drastic change, now instead of mahogany twist she now wore a neat curly afro. Of course she had to wear large silver hoops in her ears and lots of bangles for that full afro-centric affect.

Just as Kem and Sister found an empty table, the music faded out and the master of ceremony stepped to the microphone to announce the first poet of the evening. They both ordered sparkling grape juice as a nice looking young lady described in rhythm the itch she couldn't scratch. Good thing it was short Kem thought. "Some women can be so tacky" she whispered to Sister.

Next up was a really fine brother, really fine. He wore a charcoal gray t-shirt tucked into a pair of black (not too baggy and not too tight) wide leg jeans. His skin was a smooth coca brown to match the full brown lips that were producing the words driving the crowd wild. Kem heard everyone saying "Amen" and "Tell it boy" but she couldn't hear a word the man was saying; from his first word Kem was mesmerized by his voice, a deep vibrating texture that seemed to be shaking her insides. Kem had never experienced an attraction such as this. Her trance was broken by the owl calls and the snapping fingers and Sister was even standing as the young brother exited the stage.

"Ain't he bad girl?" Sister was overly excited about the guy.

"Yeah, he's bad alright. Who is he?" Kem watched him shake all the hands that were reaching out for him.

"I'll introduce you and you can thank me later." Sister waved the guy over before Kem could even begin to protest. Before she could even lick her lips, he was at their table giving Sister a 'longtime friend' hug.

"Hey ladies" the deep voice spoke.

"Keshaun this is my sister Kemiece." Sister was beaming as if she waited all her life for this moment.

"I prefer Kem, it's nice to meet you" Kem stuck out a hand she hoped wasn't sweating. A performer was on stage so he gave them respect by whispering as he took her hand and squatted next to her chair.

"His name is Keshaun Freeman" Sister whispered. "You get it? Free-man."

"What is she saying over there?" he asked.

"She's saying nothing, absolutely nothing." Kem cut her eyes at Sister.

"Do you mind if I sit with you?" Keshaun smiled a young 'Taye Diggs' kind of smile that said 'I got you don't worry.'

"Sure. I don't mind." But if he smiles like that again I'm going to be in trouble Kem thought as she watched him grab a chair from the next table and place it so close to her she couldn't imagine how he was going to sit in it.

Kem couldn't hide her blushing when Keshaun sat facing her with one long leg behind her and the other in front... well more like at an angle. Talk about giving someone your full attention. To her surprise it was something familiar about his actions; the closeness of his scent, the comfort of his thigh against her knee, but if it had been someone else, someone who wasn't smelling of sandalwood or who wasn't wearing a 'Taye Diggs' smile, or a clean shaven head with nicely trimmed sideburns and a goatee, she would have called him a pervert and politely removed herself from his presence. Keshaun, on the other hand, felt like home for some reason and she was feeling a gravitational pull in his direction so Kem sat back to enjoy the power of this man.

Sister couldn't help being tickled over her little sister's nervousness. Kemiece is normally the dominate one with strangers but tonight her sister was unfolding into Keshaun's lap. She often wondered how Kem let John get away with all the things he's done or shall she say, haven't done.

COMPATIBLE;

(Of two things) Able to exist or occur together
without conflict

Keshaun and Kem tried to include Sister in their conversation from time to time but quickly became engrossed in their own world again and again. Their compatibility seemed endless; from their favorite foods, movies, books and various other things to do, to the things that they hated, they were one in the same. They didn't agree too much on politics but they didn't disagree enough to hinder their smooth conversation.

"Haven't you all talked enough?" Keshaun had just asked Kem if she listened to talk radio when Sister rudely interrupted them and stood up. Kem wanted to shout "No and no and more no's", but by the way Keshaun and Sister were eyeing each other; she knew that her sister was up to something. There was nothing in the world that would make Sister tell something before she's ready for you to know, so Kem didn't bother to ask.

That thought put Kem in mind of their teenaged years when Sister got caught with a boy in her room; he was not only sitting on her bed but they were actually doing "It". Their father, Mr. Young, broke the barricade Sister had placed against the door just in time to see a half-naked young man jump from their second-floor window. Sister pushed herself against Mr. Young to keep him from the window and from the view of her boyfriend.

Mr. Young gave Sister a whipping every night until she revealed the boy's name. Sister took that whipping for almost two weeks before she blurted out "Malcolm Thomas". When their parents asked her why she kept it from them so long she replied: "I took a pregnancy test and I didn't want you to kill the father of my baby."

After learning her test was negative Mr. Young ordered Malcolm to come over every day for two weeks to receive the same punishment Sister had. He also added lectures on being a man and living up to your responsibilities, due to Malcolm running out on Sister leaving her to deal with him alone and to everyone's surprise, Malcolm showed up every day.

"Man! Where did everybody go?" Kem tried to change the subject.

"Were you listening the whole time?" Keshaun grabbed Sister in a playful headlock as they headed to the door.

"Quit playing. You know I was."

"So where did you park that 'Benz' of yours?" He joked.

"You mean her Lexus?" Kem joined in.

"Okay Mr. Funny man and Ms. Funny woman, you all can walk home." Sister hopped in her 94 Chevy and locked the doors.

"Sister come on, we were just playing," Kem shouted from the sidewalk while Keshaun tried to open the passenger door. Over the roaring of the engine, Kem could hear Sister shouting "Walk funny girl! Walk!" Keshaun jumped back to save his toes as Sister drove away laughing.

Kemiece could not believe her sister left her, and with a stranger at that. Kem blinked her eyes rapidly trying to see beyond Keshaun's Charm and good looks and quickly examined him for a sign of craziness. He could be a murderer or rapist or...

"Do you trust your sister?" Keshaun asked reading the worry lines on Kem's face. She thought about her sister for a moment and decided she had nothing to worry about.

"Please tell me you're driving."

"Sorry beautiful my ride just left. Do you want to take a cab, I'll ride with you? Or we can walk for a while to get to know each other." Kem gave Keshaun her hand and closed her eyes.

"Lead the way, I can use a good walk" she teased. He suggested that they walk until her legs got tired. "Are you calling me a punk?" Kem nudged him in his side.

"Naw I'm just saying that you have little feet and short legs and..."

"Short! I'm five feet six sweetie, that's hardly short." Kem let go of his hand in defiance.

"Come here lil girl" he pulled her to him and she stood nose to his chest; more like to the top of his rib cage. "Baby girl, you are short."

"That doesn't mean I'm a punk." Kem playfully pushed him and then they walked silently east towards the lake front.

Although their walk was more of a stroll they seemed to reach 51st Street pretty fast. And the cool breeze had changed to a cold chill since they started out from 43rd Street. Keshaun wanted to offer to keep Kem warm by draping his arm around her but he didn't want to scare her off.

"Want to race" he smiled, challenging her, hoping that she wouldn't say no. Kem looked down at her feet. She was wearing a pair of low heeled sandals but none that she would want to run in. "We could run in the sand. I'll even hold your shoes and your purse."

"Okay but you're going to have to let me beat you."

"And why is that?" He began to pull off his own shoes.

"What if somebody sees you? They're going to think that you robbed me for my stuff." Keshaun began to shake his head.

"I'll take my chances. You have to prove to me that you're 'not a punk' as you say."

Kem shrugged her shoulders then prepared herself for running. Keshaun watched her attempt to stretch in her tight jeans and wondered how soft her thighs were. Slow down, he told himself, touching will come soon but not tonight.

"On your mark, get set, go!" Kem shouted. Keshaun started off slowly trying to give her a head start, but she seemed to be giving him a head start. So he took off running without sympathy towards their designated finish line. Keshaun pumped his arms and his legs as hard as he could, his breathing was under control and he was feeling great when suddenly he felt a slap on his butt and a slight gust of wind blew by his ear; Kem had not only caught up with him but past him about fifty feet.

"Hurry up! Or are you trying to lose?" Kem laughed. Keshaun couldn't believe it, he willed his muscles to work overtime but they wouldn't respond. By the time he got to the finish line Kem was walking in a circle catching her breath. "I guess Sister didn't tell you that I used to run track?"

"What do you think?" Keshaun was more impressed with Kem than he was able to show. "Who did you run for?"

"Everyone" Kem smiled at his confusion. "I ran for elementary school, high school, college and the Olympics, well sort of, I sprained my ankle during tryouts."

"I guess you never went back huh?" Keshaun put his arm around Kem's shoulders to support the sadness that was overshadowing her voice. Feeling just as comfortable as he was, Kem wrapped her arm around his waist.

"No, I didn't." They walked at a slower pace enjoying the sand between their toes and the breeze that now served as a coolant to their sweaty bodies. Their conversation took them to Kem's track running days to his poetry and speech giving days. They discussed the worst jobs they ever endured to Kem's present bookstore and Keshaun's radio programs.

"What kind of topics do..."

"Hey, Kem!" A voice had interrupted Kem's question. Her assistant from the bookstore was riding piggyback on a guy Kem had seen frequently in the shop.

"Hey Stephanie, I would ask you what you're doing out here but I can already imagine." Stephanie was a wildflower. Anytime and anywhere was her motto.

Are you on your way to the African dancing?" She jumped down from her friends back and rescued her jeans from her inner thighs.

"Where about" even though he wasn't introduced Keshaun was not to be left unnoticed.

"Hi I'm Stephanie, Kem's assistant. Are you..."

"Where did you say the music was?" Kem interrupted, she was a private person. In the two years she's known Stephanie she has never mentioned or introduced any man to her. Tonight wasn't going to be any different.

"It's around 63rd Street. It's about twelve guys with bongos down there, and everybody's dancing to their music, well not everyone but it's nice." She grabbed her friends' hand as she talked. "I'll see you Monday bright and early." Stephanie laughed at that last comment because she knew there was no such thing as 'bright and early' in her book.

"Interesting" Keshaun said. Kem thought that she was in for an argument about not introducing him so she braced herself for more. "Let's go check it out." He grabbed her hand and pulled her towards the music. Kem released a breath of relief and gladly followed. They were near Fifty-Fifth Street, so a few more blocks wouldn't hurt.

Feeling the rhythm vibrating in the air rejuvenated them as they approached the crowd. Keshaun had started swaying to the music as he walked and Kem was snapping her fingers to the beat. The crowd that gathered was singing "Go brother go brother" over and over to an elderly guy dancing within the circle of bongos. He spotted Kem and motioned for her to join him; even if she tried the crowd wouldn't let her decline.

Keshaun was proud of her sportsmanship and he was becoming more and more amazed with this woman. Her movements were graceful and provocative at the same time. Keshaun felt as though she was dancing for him; her hips swayed with the music and easily changed directions with every strike of the drum, begging him to touch them.

With eyes closed, Kem was in a zone; the music was her audience and every pop of her hip and drop of her butt released stress and emotional pain that had built up inside of her. Not until the crowd started barking did she realize that Keshaun had joined her. He was following her every move from behind her; one hand on the side of her thigh and another pressed against her stomach guiding her and begging her to flow to his motion. And so she did, swayed when he swayed, dipped when he dipped. She was beginning to feel dizzy, in a good way.

Kem's arms had nowhere to go but up and behind Keshaun's neck. He bent lower and snuggled into her neck, a perfect fit he thought. Her body next to his was warm and soft and to his surprise he didn't have a hard on. He sent a secret message of gratitude to his manhood for behaving. He wanted this woman, he needed this woman. She was beautiful, intelligent, and fun and business oriented. Just what the doctor ordered so it was no wonder why his next move came so naturally.

"Do you realize you just kissed me?" Kem turned to face him. The closeness they shared was not of two people just meeting but of two souls touching each other, finding a home.

"Did I?" Keshaun was more than aware of his actions and the gloss on her lips made him want to taste them. He kissed her lips firmly with the inner portion of his lips mentally tying his tongue to his throat for they were still in the mist of the crowd and getting slapped in front of a lot of people has never been a fantasy of his. The smile she gave him after he released her lips let him know that he had done nothing wrong. "Are you hungry?"

INTOXICATING;

Excite or exhilarate. Buzz, thrill.

Sunday morning came in fast and heavy. The wind was blowing hot air everywhere and Kem's ceiling fan was on full blast and even though she'd already removed her t-shirt and the shorts she'd dressed in that morning, she couldn't feel a thing. Hanging out with Keshaun was so intoxicating that it now felt like a hangover. Kem didn't want to move, not even to turn on the air conditioner but now her phone was ringing.

"Yes may I help you?" Kem had crawled out of bed to retrieve the phone from her vanity table. She hated to answer the phone while she was sleeping because she would never remember the conversation, so placing the phone away from the bed was the best way to wake up just enough to control that matter.

"Put your mama on the phone"

"What." Kem was confused.

"Yeah, this me, I'm never coming home again." Keshaun was laughing at his poor attempt to recite a line from the movie "Harlem Nights".

"Oh, so am I "Sunshine"?"

"Yes, you are" Keshaun's smile floated through the phone lines and landed in her lap. Everything about him made her feel like a kid again, not that she was even close to being old but Keshaun made her feel giddy. "How fast can you get dressed?"

"Honestly?"

"Ok, you're right" he said. "Just get dressed, I want to take you somewhere" Keshaun hung up and Kem began to feel like a kid, who was going to the circus for the first time, as she rummaged through her closet for something to wear. Not knowing the destination, made getting dressed an absolute challenge but the white denim jeans and the white blouse that she chose, seem to be perfect with her red sandals and red bangles.

Kem was getting exciting chills from her goose bumps and watching Keshaun's strides from her window, as he walked up to her building, made her stomach tremble.

"Hey there" Keshaun smiled as he entered the apartment.

"Hey yourself"

"You look beautiful" Keshaun took Kem's hand and spun her around. "Do you have an iron?"

"Why, am I wrinkled" Kem looked herself over; she did iron her clothes pretty quick but she didn't think that she missed anything.

"Yeah, all that" Keshaun laughed and took his shirt off, uncovering a chest that Kem was going to dream about touching for the next few hours.

"Ok, so you're a comedian too." Kem lead Keshaun to the extra bedroom where she kept her iron and ironing board. They looked each other over in silence as the iron heated up and their emotions stirred up. Kem looked away first, grabbing Keshaun's t-shirt from his hand and began to iron it. Before she could even give it three strokes, Keshaun gently took the iron from her. "You're going too slow, taking your pretty time." Even that made Kem smile; his rudeness was even cute, she laughed to herself.

Kem and Keshaun talked about friends and siblings as he drove them, in his Corvette down Lake Shore Drive, to their destination. Asking him where they were going didn't even cross Kem's mind because for some reason, she trusted him and enjoyed his masculine guidance; his assertion and confidence was something wonderful to watch. Keshaun never came off cocky to her and he was always, even in the least bit, considerate of whatever she wanted.

"Here we are" Keshaun sung out as he parked the car outside of Lincoln Park Zoo. The zoo, a place that Kem would have never, in a million years, guessed he would take her. "I figured that you were the 'zoo' type of date" he smiled. Kem didn't know how to take that comment. Why couldn't she be the 'introduce to the friend, hang out kind of date' or the 'steak house kind of date' or the...

"What's wrong" Keshaun was trying to read Kem's face.

"The zoo kind of date?" She asked and waited for him to explain.

"It's better than being the hotel kind" he simply said. Although Kem wanted to be fully intimate with him, he was right. Kem had been the hotel, his house, his car, and her house kind of date more times than she'd wish to remember.

"Yeah you're right" Kem agreed out loud. Keshaun smiled again, grabbed her hand and lead her to the most wonderful two hours she'd ever spent, outdoors, with a man. The following week wasn't short of awesome either; they went bicycle riding along the lake, played volleyball in the sand with a group of strangers and today they were going to the pool before dinner. Keshaun was slowly stirring cool-aid while Kem grilled chicken breast, both daydreaming about that moment when they could no longer stop their kisses from going to a place they both wanted to be but didn't want to scare the other one away.

"You never cease to amaze me."

"What do you mean? And thank you by the way." Kem was again, smiling from ear to ear. Keshaun explained how he was impressed with her business, her cooking and "just everything". Kem couldn't take her eyes off of his lips as he spoke to her; they seemed to beckon to her and she couldn't help but to glide over to him. Before she could stop herself, she was standing in front of him, gliding her hands up his arms to the back of his neck, pulling him towards her.

"What kind of party is this turning into?" Keshaun said as he kissed her, long and deep. He lifted her as if she weighed nothing and carried her over to the sofa, lowering her gently. Every time that they took a breath from kissing, Keshaun hugged her tightly, looked down at her and then kissed her again. "We'll never get out of here like this." Keshaun got up and softly pulled Kem to her feet. Kem could care less about swimming at that point and by Keshaun's erection, she knew that he wanted more too but Kem guessed, just like she, Keshaun was well aware of their timing.

After playing in the pool, dinner and watching a movie on the sofa, Keshaun told her that he was flying out to Atlanta in the morning for a radio show and that she was going to be his first priority when he touched back down in Chicago. "Now don't go falling in love with someone else before I get back."

"I won't," Kem said with every intention to only think of him and their time together but "Murphy's Law" had other plans.

Murphy's Law

"If something can go wrong, it will, and usually at the worst time"

Four days had passed since Keshaun had left and she and Keshaun's week did replay, over and over, just as she had planned but just as she noticed a pair of John's shorts in the laundry that she was folding, her phone began to ring, pulling her from her daydream. "Hello".

"May I come in?" Kem heard the voice and she had heard the words but the question wasn't making any since. "Kem, can you come open the door?" It was John and he was at her door.

"I can't talk to you right now I have to get ready for worship service."

"You must be going to evening service because it's three in the afternoon." He had the nerve to laugh. Kem pressed the number six button on the telephone to buzz John into the building. She then stumbled over the bad mood he was now putting her in and re-dressed into her t-shirt and shorts she'd discarded when the warm Sunday sun began to beam through her window. When she opened her door John was wearing a goofy grin and carrying a large grocery bag.

"What do you want John?" and what's the bag for she wanted to ask but she didn't want to appear too interested.

"I came to cook dinner for you." John brushed past her and headed towards the kitchen. Kem closed the door and observed her reflection in the mirror. Her boy shorts appeared too short and she was in much need of a bra. Suddenly feeling naked Kem rushed to her room and grabbed her robe, still not satisfied she decided to get dressed completely. She grabbed her yoga pants from the end of her bed, her bra hanging from her doorknob and ran into the bath room. Why was she feeling this way? John's seen her naked a million times.

"Kemiece what are you doing?" John was starting to rattle pans and Kem's nerves at the same time.

"I'll be out in a moment." She yanked her arms out of her sleeves and let her t-shirt swing from her neck while she fastened her bra. Kem reluctantly brushed her teeth and gargled with mouth wash. She could still taste and feel Keshaun's kisses and she was hoping the feeling would last until he got back. She silently prayed that John wouldn't kiss her... or touch her for that matter; her skin still tingled from Keshaun's touch. Oh that man was powerful she thought and John's presence was invading her space, her emotions and everything else.

Kem finished dressing and joined John in the kitchen. John grabbed her and kissed her firmly on the lips. He tried to reach for her tongue but for some reason Kem didn't share the same desire. "I missed you so much," he said then returned to his work. Being with Keshaun was so comfortable that Kem didn't think of John at all, Keshaun didn't even ask if she was seeing any one. Maybe he didn't care. But why wouldn't he care? Does he have someone himself? No that wouldn't be it because Sister said he was a 'free man' and she trusted her sister. Maybe Keshaun believed that his charm was so powerful that she would drop anybody that she was dating to be with him. Ok, now she was making excuses for her present company. Keshaun was just confident and natural and probably knew that no one could make her feel the way he does so she'd be a fool to let someone come between...

"What are you smiling about?"

"I was smiling?" Kem opened the freezer door to veil her face. She couldn't stand in the freezer forever so she grabbed the ice tray and closed the door.

"Yes, you were smiling. What were you thinking about?" John stopped what he was doing to let her know that he wanted a response.

"I um... was just thinking that you have never cooked for me." He smiled and returned to chopping whatever he was chopping. "What's up with that? Are you trying to prove something?" Kem asked playfully but she seriously wanted to know his game plan.

"I'm a changed man and it's time I start showing you that I'm authentic. I know my words don't mean much to you anymore so I decided to do something different." John turned to look at Kem hoping that she believed him but she didn't even seem concerned with why he hadn't called in two weeks or why he didn't show up that Friday and as long as she didn't ask, he wasn't going to tell.

Kem wanted to believe him but at this moment her thoughts were tumbled, she didn't even know if it mattered anymore. She had to say something but she could only think of asking him if he'd moved out yet. So she said nothing, well nothing that pertained to them anyway.

"Do you need any help?" Kem retrieved a glass from the cabinet and filled it with ice and water. John looked a little disappointed but he pushed his thoughts aside.

"No. I can handle it." John went back to cooking and Kem escaped to the living room and her Sunday paper. By the time John called her to dinner; Kem had read the whole front portion of the paper, the entertainment and arts section, the comics and she'd done two crossword puzzles. She was beginning to appreciate the aroma that was coming from her kitchen because the breakfast bar that she had several hours ago been long gone.

As she entered the dining room she began to feel under dressed. John had placed a floral center piece on the table and surrounded it with candles of various sizes. There were dinner rolls, salads and glasses of red wine at two place settings.

"I'm impressed. You know a little some-some huh?" Kem sat down as John placed a steaming hot plate of sea food linguine in front of her. He placed a finger under her chin, raised it to him and kissed her.

"Everything is going to get better." John statement made Kem feel guilty. Here she was hanging out with another man while her man was thinking of her and planning to make their relationship better. So many words were running through her mind at this time; guilt: fact of having committed a specified or implied offense, weak minded: mentally deficient lacking in resolution, and obligation: constraining power of a law, precept, duty, contract, binding agreement, a service or benefit, indebtedness, responsibility, charge, burden; trust, liability; see also KINDNESS.

"Aren't you going to answer your phone?"

"What?"

"Kem your phone is ringing." John jumped up and went into the living room. "Hello! Yeah I guess you do." He came back into the dining room and placed the phone next to Kem. "I wouldn't want you to miss another call." John's voice was daring and traced with a hint of jealously, it was almost funny to Kem.

"You have changed" Kem smiled at him. John knew exactly what she was talking about. He has never displayed any emotion or interest in her callers or who she would spend her time with when he wasn't around. This was a change that Kem was going to enjoy. Now that John was fully aware that he wasn't the only man who wanted her attention Kem felt empowered.

POWERED;

Capacity, capability, ability, potential, competence, potentiality, dominance, mastery, rule, command, ascendancy, sovereignty, dominion; weight, sway, pull (clout).

You know the funniest thing about power is that you have to know how to use it and hold it when you think you've got it. When you lay it up on the shelf, waiting for the perfect time to bring it out, the perfect time to say "It's time you moved out of that house", it could be too late. Your power could begin to evaporate and your most powerful words could end up sounding like;

"Baby don't you think it's time to move out of that house and get your own space."

"It's coming baby. You have to be a little more patient." John answered much too quickly. He must have been waiting for her to ask that question Kem thought. It has been two weeks and two days since she'd gained her so called power. Now her energy to muster up patience was as powerful as a year old tic-tac.

"Come on now Kemiece. I've been here at least four nights this week."

"I guess I should be grateful right." Kem swung her legs to the side of her bed and sat up. Her robe was too far away at the moment so she just sat there naked searching for truth.

"I didn't say that." John rolled over towards her and began rubbing her shoulders. "Just give me a little more time. We could even get a place together if you like. But you have to let me do this my way." He rolled back onto the bed and turned on the TV. The conversation was over, just like her power. Just like her chances to be with Keshaun, just like her life.

Why not wait for John? "I've waited this long" she thought out loud. What did she have to lose that she haven't lost already. She's ignored enough of Keshaun's calls to make him forget her for three lifetimes. And what did she owe him anyway? They spent one week together, one beautiful sexless week and several intimate kisses that she can still feel across her lips. Does that mean anything?

He's a grown man he couldn't possible think... or feel... exactly how she feel. Could he? Kem slowly crawled back into bed and pulled the sheets up to her neck feeling... she didn't know what she was feeling. Kem could think of many words but the word discontent seemed to stand out in the crowd.

PERFECT;

Blameless Complete; not deficient. Faultless; in morals or behavior

Wednesday and a hump day it was; Kem's book store "Page Turner" was buzzing beyond control. Ever since she added live jazz on Wednesdays it seemed as the whole Hyde Park community would fall in for a taste, not to mention the book signing that was taking place today.

Shameek, an up and coming novelist, would be arriving in less than an hour. His book cover, picturing a light skinned brother with long curly hair, a well-toned torso partially covered by an opened vest, alone was enough to bring any female into the store. His jeans were slightly baggy accompanied by a pair of unlaced Timberland boots. The title over Shameek self- portrait read "Brother on a Come Back."

Whatever, Kem thought, but by the looks of the line of women forming outside, her thoughts stood alone. Kem just hoped the book signing went well, the band played well, the coffee tasted great and that she'd be able to close no more than a half hour late. John was coming over for dinner and she wanted everything to be perfect and on time.

Through the front window Kem noticed a pregnant woman standing in line. She looked as if shifting from one foot to the other wasn't enough to handle the pressure her belly was creating. So Kem had her assistant bring a chair to the front of the store and place it next to the signing table while she stepped outside.

"Miss, hi I have a chair inside for you if you'd like." Kem held the door for the wobbling lady as she made her way to the front of the line. Kem could hear the disapproving crowd by the smacking of their lips.

"Oh, girl thanks. I didn't know how much longer I could wait for this Shameek brother. What does that mean anyway?"

"I have no idea, but by the looks of the line outside I'd say no one cares." Kem smiled as she offered the woman a cup of water. "Enjoy and let me know if you need anything."

"I will. Thanks." The woman replied just as the keys she was holding dropped to the floor. Kem retrieved them but froze in mid motion. On one of the key rings held a portrait of John in a tux beaming down at his beautiful bride, whom was now sitting before Kem reaching out for her keys with a swollen belly.

"Are you okay?" the woman asked Kem's confused expression.

"Umm... yes, I'm fine. He just looks like someone I know." Kem stood, handed over the keys and hoped hatred wasn't written on her face; not for the woman but for John.

"Who John, you probably know him from here in your store; he buys my books from here all the time."

"I guess so." Kem quickly excused herself for the nausea setting in wasn't going to wait for privacy. She quickly retreated to her office and closed the door. "That lying son of a..." Kem stopped herself from ranting and thought for a moment, breathe Kem she told herself. Think! Think! Think! She listened to the ticking of the clock on her wall and sat down.

"Not telling your mate everything, everything important, is the same as telling them a lie. If you're withholding information that can affect their future, it is a lie. If..."

The radio relationship expert was yet again getting on Kem's nerve. Why is his segment on every time she needs to hear the... truth? Kemiece pressed the off button on the remote. "He didn't actually lie" but being deceitful is close enough she thought and shouldn't she know that the man, that she is planning to be patient for is about to have a brand new baby with a wife he says he's divorcing and what kind of woman would she be if she lets him. She decided to call John to ask him if the baby was his. She wanted to listen to his voice, hear him say no or maybe or something that would release the vise-grip from around her throat.

Kem was just about to dial John's number when Stephanie's voice came over the intercom letting her know that Shameek had arrived. "I'll be out in a moment," Kem said pulling herself together. She dabbed on some lip gloss, tucked her blouse into her jeans and put on her blazer. She would get through this day if it killed her. When the bulk of the crowd is gone she'll come back into the office, call John and let him have it, but right now she will be the perfect host to all her guest, save one.

AILING;

In poor health, unwell, indisposed, delicate, weak

Sister held her nose as she entered Kem's apartment, trying not to lose the breakfast she'd just eaten. Sister followed the stench to the kitchen, where she found take out packages overflowing the counter and the kitchen table. The Chinese food, pizza, ice cream and seafood particles were very identifiable. Sister placed the few dishes that were in the sink into the dish washer, she then filled a cherry red tea kettle with water, turned on the burner and placed a bag of chamomile tea inside a large ceramic mug.

"Hey, girl" Sister tried to sound cheerful as she entered Kem's bedroom. Kem was lying faced down with her blanket over her head and her pillows were trailing from the bed to the bedroom door. The clothes Kem wore Wednesday were thrown over a lounge chair and a pile of men's clothes were sitting by the window. "Kemiece" Sister shouted. Kem threw the covers off of her head; Sister smiled knowing that would get a response from her sister.

"What do you want Sister?" Kem mumbled into her bed sheets.

"I came to see if you were alive. You weren't answering the phone."

"It was too far away." Kem pointed in the direction she threw her phone after she hung up on John three days ago.

"Well, look at that. It is far away." Sister joked spotting the cell phone near the bathroom door.

"Look I am not in the..." Kem tried shouting but Sister put her hand over her mouth.

"I'm sorry sweetie. I didn't come over to upset you." Sister slowly removed her hand to see if Kem had calmed down. Kem resumed her position under her blanket. "Would you like some breakfast and a nice warm bath? I can hook you up." Sister waited but Kem said nothing. So she eased out of the room and softly closed the door.

Kem could hear pots and pans rattling in the kitchen; the noise disturbed and pleased her at the same time. She appreciated a big sister who knew how to take care of her when she wasn't in the mood to take care of her own ailing mentality. "Sister" Kem called out from the steaming hot water that was beginning to sooth her aching soul and tug at her tears. She was glad for the presence of steam by the time Sister came into the bathroom.

"Don't tell me you're in here crying" Nothing could get passed Sister or maybe she knew that there was plenty of reasons why she should be crying; three years of forgiving excuses that she knew were lies, three years of giving of herself and other things that John had no intentions of returning. "You can cry if you want to, it's your party" Sister laughed at her terrible humor.

"Sister why are you alone? Why aren't you letting some man make you happy" Kem asked hoping Sister didn't take it the wrong way.

"Who said I didn't have anyone to make me happy? My situation is complicated to the romantic ear."

"What do you mean, who is this invisible man?" Kem looked a bit worried but intrigued at the same time.

"Let me ask you this first, does John make you smile even though he's not around? Don't look at me like that... you know what I mean." Sister held back laughing at Kem's face when she mentioned John's name. Kem thought for a moment and shook her head 'no'. "Ok, when you were at your happiest moment with him, did you get lost in time where nothing else mattered; not time, not work or even the people around you?"

"Well damn" Kem chuckled but she honestly couldn't say yes to that question either, however, she did get lost in Keshaun when she was with him. "No".

"Well, that's the kind of relationship that I'm in with my guy." Sister paused and smiled to herself. "He's gentle, considerate and our lovemaking is precise and when we're together... no one else exists."

"Sister, he's not married is he?" Kem couldn't believe her ears, Sister was seeing a married man above all the advice that she has ever given her, and she herself was walking a thin line.

"It's difficult to explain but yes, for ten years I've been completely in love with Isaac White, Baltimore-born. And what we have I wouldn't trade for the world for fear that the feelings wouldn't be the same.

"But..."

"I know I preach to you about having a 'free-man' because that is what 'you' need. John doesn't make you happy and he never will... I'm not trying to offend you baby sister but I think that you only stayed with him because you were able to predict his actions and if you hadn't found out about the new baby, you'd still be willing to work it out." Sister paused again to softly deliver her next few words. "I believe, deep down, that you knew that John was married all along."

Kem lowered herself deeper into the bathtub; the truth was heavy. "Isaac has never made me feel like I was second or even shared him with anyone for that matter. He's never disrespected me in anyway and I am never lonely. Before my smile could even begin to fade away, he's at my doorstep or on the line saying 'hey Ms. Wet wet' or something equally charming" Sister laughed.

"I don't even want to know what he means by 'wet wet'" Kem laughed as she began to sit up again, moving her butt around that was beginning to stick to the tub. "Well, I must say, you are always happy, unless you are secretly crying at night." They both laughed.

"Not ever" Sister said walking towards the bathroom door. "Do me a favor and just think of someone who makes you smile, even when they're not around. That's it, just think about them."

"What if I've never made love to this person? Is it possible to actually love them?"

"There's more to love, than making love." Sister headed towards the kitchen on that note, leaving Kem to ponder in the now 'luke warm' bath water. Could she possibly have more feelings for Keshaun in these few short weeks than she has for John? She did think of Keshaun every moment that she was with John and their time together felt like they were living in a world of their own. Kem couldn't even remember if there were kids at the swimming pool when they were there, oblivious to the world. She must admit that it felt pretty good to smile about how someone was making her feel.

"Here's your robe" Sister smiled mischievously. "Your breakfast is on your nightstand, and I'll call you later."

"Ok, I love you" Kem barely got the words out before she heard her bedroom door close. The luke-warm water began to sooth her thoughts as she scooped it with her hands and let it fall over the exposed parts of her body. Every drop seem to release a bit of stress as it rolled down into the tub to reunited with the rest of her bath water.

Kem took a long look in the mirror and thought about Keshaun; his smile, his laugh and how he calls her 'lil girl,' making her smile for days. "Time to put on my big girl panties," Kem said to her reflection and then she put on her robe and walked into her bedroom to find her cell phone. On her bed next to her nightstand sat Keshaun Freeman and for the first time, he looked unsure of his actions.

"Hey there," his smile was light.

"Hey you" Kem slowly walked over and sat next to Keshaun; heart pounding uncontrollably, breathing needed calming but she was ready for whatever he had to say. "I'd like to explain..."

"Not right now," Keshaun said grabbing her plate off of the nightstand. He waited for Kem to acknowledge that he was serious and for her to sit back onto the bed. "Your grits are getting cold and I'm not cooking anymore" he laughed.

"What do you mean by 'anymore'? Have you been here the whole time… cooking?" Kem hoped he wasn't listening in on her and Sister. She was going to kill Sister.

"Don't worry, I didn't hear a word; I don't want to know anything that you don't want to tell me but right now I just want you to eat." Kem was about to say something else but Keshaun began to feed her eggs and grits.

Keshaun fed Kem every morsel on her plate, tighten her robe and helped her back into bed. Then he placed her plate onto the floor next to the bed and crawled into bed behind Kem, wrapping his arms around her.

"Keshaun"

"Yes lil girl" Keshaun smiled at Kem's giggling.

"I love your radio program" Kem smiled at how shocked she was to learn that Keshaun was the relationship expert that helped her over the last couple of days. Instead of turning her radio off, she turned the volume up. And although she thought that he was talking directly to her, it made her feel better to know that she wasn't the only woman out there who had 'borrowed love'.

"Kem, wake up. Don't you know what can happen when a person fall asleep in the tub?" Sister stood over Kem with a horrified look on her face. "People drown in tubs is what they do." Kem looked at Sister puzzled; her bath water was cold and soap scum had built up around her shoulders. How long had it been since she dozed off? Why did Keshaun feel so real?

"I had this dream, it felt so real." Kem gasped. "Is Keshaun the relationship expert on the radio?"

"I was wondering when you were going to figure that out."

Kem reached down into the water, pulled the stopper out and then turned on the shower to wash the soap scum off of her body. She should have known that a man like Keshaun wouldn't have come back into her life so easily. She'd messed up, trying to hold on to someone that she was... used to instead of venturing forward.

"I hope you know that I'm still expecting you to help with my party tonight." Sister yelled as she headed towards the kitchen.

"Has he asked about me?"

"Has who asked about you?"

"Sister who else could I be referring to? Has Keshaun said anything to you, about me?" Kem was wrapping a towel around her body as she followed Sister into the kitchen. She hated Sister's playful timing. Didn't she know that she was desperate right now?

"Well, ask him yourself, at the party tonight." Sister grabbed her purse and pointed towards an overloaded garbage bag. "I cooked and cleaned but you have to take out your own trash. Your food is in the microwave." She kissed Kem on her forehead, turned and started singing as she left Kem's apartment.

"If I can't have you, I don't want nobody baby..." Her sister's voice trailed off as she closed the door behind her. Kem looked at the clock on the microwave and inwardly screamed; Sister's party was in five hours and she had no idea what to wear.

She had originally decide on something cute enough to be comfortable in and not make John insecure, where he felt that he had to watch her all night. Now, there was a change of plans; there was no John and she needed something super sexy, weighing on the edge of "I'm available" but not to everyone. She had to go shopping.

Relationship;

The way in which two or more concepts, objects or people are connected, or the state of being connected.

The banquet hall was elegantly set; Kem and a few of Sister's friends worked fast and hard to decorate after Kem was done shopping. Kem was able to run home, get dressed and make it back before Sister's grand entrance, alone. The thought saddened Kem; how could Sister be so content being alone on a night like this. Maybe mystery man was hiding in the shadows Kem laughed to herself as she looked around the room for a man with the widest grin on his face and possibly a three piece suit to match Sister's dress.

Kem's smile faded as her eyes landed on John's silly grin, sitting at the bar. She'd forgotten to un-invite him to the party. John nodded his head towards her and then began to order something from the bartender. "Lord please, don't let him buy me a drink" Kem thought in horror. Kem quickly turned her attention towards the dance floor which was more horrifying. Keshaun was on the dance floor dancing with someone looking as though he had never met her. He looked happy, unaffected by her desertion.

Kem quickly grabbed her purse and started searching for... something to take her attention off of Keshaun. Her heart was pounding and she was beginning to feel a sense of loneliness when someone tapped her on her shoulder.

"Would you like to dance?" John asked almost as if he knew she wouldn't say no, grabbing her purse and placing it on the table. Kem let him help her up, but grabbed her purse and walked in the opposite direction of the dance floor, never looking back. She headed towards the food table hoping John wasn't following her. He was.

"Are you avoiding me?" John stepped in front of her at the food table.

"Would you please go away? You shouldn't even be here." Kem began to tell the server what she wanted, gently pushing John aside.

"I thought that you might want to see me."

"You thought that..." Kem couldn't bring herself to continue. She grabbed her plate from the server and headed back to her table. John had a lot of nerve she thought. Did he really think that she wasn't over him?

Was she? Kem looked around the room as John sat down next to her as if he belonged there. It seemed as if everyone was watching them and she'd hoped that Keshaun wasn't. Kem frantically searched the room for Sister.

"You know that you're going to always belong to me, I don't know why you're acting like this," John said smugly, picking up a piece of chicken from Kem's plate.

"I will never belong to you" Kem tried to scoot her chair away from John but he grabbed her chair with one hand and grabbed the back of her neck with the other, pulling her towards him. His breath was hot with liquor against Kem's face as he spoke.

"Do you really think that you can live without me?"

"You're hurting my neck, John," Kem whispered, trying not to draw embarrassing attention to them; trying not to cry. John was supposed to love her but here he was, abusing her physically and mentally, in a room full of people. Kem wanted to fight back but she didn't want to ruin Sister's party. She tried to think of something as tears started to flow from the corners of her eyes and her leg began to nervously twitch. John's lips were brushing against her cheek and his hand groped her thighs as he continued to talk. Kem squeezed her eyes shut, wishing him away.

"Yeah, you better... "John's voice faded out as his hands seemed to quickly move away from Kem. Kem thought that maybe something harsher was coming her way, like a slap but when a few seconds passed and nothing happened, she opened her eyes to find John being held up by his collar by a man in a three piece suit while Keshaun was nose to nose with him, giving him harsh instructions to leave the premises. John nodded his understanding and the man with the three-piece suit let him go with a push and John landed on the floor. John got up holding on to his gut and ran out of the banquet hall.

Kem began to softly sob with relief as Sister sat next to her rubbing her back. "It's all over... Shh," Sister said over and over until her sobs lighten.

"I ruined your party."

"Honey, no you did not" Sister laughed. "If anything ruins my party it would be that ugly face of yours. You're getting snot all over your pretty new dress." Kem began to cry again. "I was just kidding, stop crying."

"I got her, go back to your party." Keshaun helped Sister up and then sat down next to Kem handing her a cool towel. Sister looked back to see if Kem was ok before latching onto the man in the three-piece suit and heading towards the dance floor. "Would you like to take a walk with me?" Kem looked up at Keshaun wondering why he wanted to put up with her and how she was ever going to thank him for helping her. "Don't worry about it," he said reading her thoughts.

Keshaun took his suit jacket off and draped it around Kem's shoulders when they got outside. The air was brisk but comforting at the same time. They walked silently towards the large water fountain with golden statues of baby angels spewing water from their mouths. They began to circle the fountain, watching the lights change colors every few seconds, listening to the rocks crunch beneath their feet with their every step.

"He's never done that before" Kem said, stopping to look at Keshaun for the first time. She felt the need to let him know that she wasn't that type of woman; to put up with abuse. Kem didn't want that kind of judgment from him or from anyone for that matter.

"I wasn't thinking that. Kem, you're beautiful and smart and any man would be afraid to lose you." Keshaun grabbed Kem's hand, prompting her to continue walking. "He was just scared that it was finally over for you two, that's all."

"Are you defending him now?"

"I would never do that. I just know a little something about relationships." Keshaun smiled.

"So I've heard" Kem smiled with him. "So tell me, what would a man, such as you, do with a woman like me in a situation such as this?" Keshaun stopped walking, turned to face Kem and pulled her so close to him that his lips brushed her ear, sending tingles down her spine.

"A man, such as me, would... ask you to race him." Keshaun laughed stepping back to look Kem over. She smiled, wanting to kiss him. "But with that tight dress on and those short legs, I'd have to give you a ten minute head start."

"Ten minutes! If I remember correctly, you're the one who needed a head start" Kem laughed. Keshaun pulled her close again and kissed her. His lips were cool at first but then heat began to rise from everywhere, leaving Kem feeling weak when Keshaun finally released her mouth.

No other words were needed from either of them. Kem knew that she wouldn't want to spend another day without Keshaun and Keshaun knew that he was going to have to take his time with her. Kem was emotionally delicate but he knew exactly what she needed; him.

THE END

CPSIA information can be obtained
at www.ICGtesting.com
Printed in the USA
LVHW091327240821
695989LV00003B/83

9 781984 572455